BELIEVE: 13 HAUNTINGS

Believe: 13 Hauntings

Elisabeth Wathen

Contents

Ghosts are all around us. Look for them,
and you will find them.
-Ruskin Bond

They say that shadows of deceased ghosts
Do haunt the houses and the graves about,
Of such whose life's lamp went untimely out,
Delighting still in their forsaken hosts.
-Joshua Sylvester

A house is never still in darkness to those who listen intently; there is a whispering in distant chambers, an unearthly hand presses the snib of the window, the latch rises. Ghosts were created when the first man woke in the night.
— J.M. Barrie

DEDICATION

For any who, like me, cling to a belief in something more, and thus
are drawn to ghosties, ghoulies and things that go bump in the night.
And for friends and family who have loyally endured countless
haunted walks & tours whenever and wherever we go together,
throughout the years.

1

NO SUCH THING AS GHOSTS

Tory waited beside the two bikes they'd stowed behind a gigantic magnolia tree, wondering what was taking Rob so long. She'd said good night to her parents, waited until she heard them go to bed themselves, and then, at 11:30, climbed out her bedroom window, tiptoed along the roof, and jumped down onto the mossy, leaf-strewn side yard, silent as a cat. The magnolia tree was half a block away, and she was there at 11:45, just as Rob had asked.

"Fine, *fine*, I'll go with you. But we don't tell *anyone*," Tory made him swear. She'd had all she could take, listening day after day to him going on about this latest fascination. Finally, it occurred to her that maybe if she gave in and went along, he'd let it go.

They were going ghost hunting.

Rob had been obsessed for almost a year. Ever since he'd stumbled across the "Supernatural Nature" podcast last winter, he couldn't seem to get enough. He'd listened to every episode, practically had them all memorized. He'd bought books about haunted places, "true" ghost stories. He'd got himself a Ouija board and tried to conduct his own séances. Lately he'd been begging his parents to take him to New Orleans, which in his mind was spook central in North America.

Tory was sick and tired of it. So this was her solution: go along on the ghost hunting thing he'd been bugging her about, prove to him that

1

he's wrong. She was determined to prove to him that there's no such thing as ghosts and drag him off this new hobbyhorse once and for all.

At midnight she finally heard footsteps, and there he was.

"What took you so long? I was about to give up and go back home!"

"Sorry," he pointed at the backpack slung over one shoulder. "I had some trouble figuring out how to pack up the snacks." She had made it clear that good snacks were part of the deal. He reached back with his other arm to get the pack firmly in place. "Ready?"

Tory indicated her own backpack, which contained candles, matches and a notebook for recording what happened, all the things he'd asked her to bring. "Let's do this."

They pulled out the bikes and sped off.

Rob had explained that their timing was perfect: November was a good time for contacting the spirit world, and this particular Saturday night was ideal because there was no moon. According to his research, moonless nights were the best for hauntings.

"Also," he went on excitedly as they'd walked home from school on Friday afternoon, "after midnight, usually around 2 a.m., is the best time; it should be easy for us to wait for our folks to go to sleep before we sneak out and get there in plenty of time. By 5:00 any shot at seeing anything is gone, so we'll be back before sunrise for sure. They'll never know we were gone."

"What are the candles for?" Tory wanted to know. "Why not just bring a flashlight?"

"I am," Rob told her. "But supernatural forces can affect electricity and make batteries die. Plus, there are tons of accounts of candle flames turning blue when a ghostly presence is near, so the candles are also a kind of early warning system for us." He'd told her a lot more, too: about how ghosts and haunted places are always cold, and many people report a sense of being mesmerized, sometimes even frozen in place, when they witness a haunting. "You should be prepared for anything to happen," he cautioned her, "but not so scared that you run away. The whole idea here is that we both witness the same thing at the same time: *proof* that it's real."

She felt a little guilty that in *her* mind, the whole idea was exactly the opposite. But only a little. She reasoned that she was really doing her best friend a favor, waking him up to reality.

Pedaling fast to keep warm in the cold night air. There was no question in her mind that they would not see anything tonight; the question was, would his embarrassment over the failure make him give up on this stuff, or at least shut up about it? That's what she was hoping, and she wasn't above laying it on thick afterward. Not that she wanted to hurt him, not really; she just wanted him to stop obsessing over this stuff. It wasn't much fun to be around him anymore. She wanted her best friend back, for things to be like they used to be.

Suburban neighborhoods gave way to wooded stretches of road interspersed with swampy lowlands and rolling, fallow farmland. A dirt road broke away at a sharp angle, and they followed it until, passing a thick stand of pines, they pulled up to a cleared patch of land with a dilapidated shack just visible at the opposite corner, tucked into some woods on the far side.

They paused there together, squinting through the darkness, starlight the only thing that pushed back the shadows.

"It looks so sad, forgotten," Tory breathed. "Isn't this near one of the old slave burial grounds? There ought to be one of those historic markers around here. Why doesn't someone take care of this place?"

Rob just shrugged. "Money, I guess. And who would come and visit it, so that it matters?" He made a grim face and put his feet back on the pedals of his bike. "I don't think many people like remembering what this place stands for."

It only took them three or four minutes to negotiate the bumpy field and pull up to the old house. Tory was surprised at how large it was. From the road it had looked more like a cabin, but up close she realized it was three stories tall, bigger than her own house.

"Let's park the bikes over by that tree," Rob whispered.

As soon as they had stowed their bikes, Rob took out his flashlight. "Just to be sure we don't step on any rotten floorboards or anything," he said as he led the way up the grey wood stairs and across the porch.

The front door was ajar, although there was no glass in any of the windows, so they could've easily gotten inside even if it'd been locked. Tory followed Rob as he walked through all the halls and rooms of the first floor. Here and there a piece of wooden furniture rotted away, but for the most part the rooms were only populated with desiccating piles of leaves and evidence of animals. One room had signs of people: some old beer cans, a broken bottle, and what looked like the remains of a fire in the fireplace. But it was old, and nowhere did they see any hints of anyone having been there recently.

"Good," Rob nodded with satisfaction. "Now we have to check out upstairs, and then find some place to wait."

"Okay."

"We have to find the *right* place. We'll know it when we *feel* it," he whispered, and glanced over his shoulder at her. "It's a sense you get, according to everything I've read. Maybe it'll be colder than any of the other rooms. Maybe you'll get goose bumps, or the hairs on the back of your neck will stand up. Maybe you'll feel an overpowering emotion that doesn't make sense— we can't predict what it'll be; we'll just *know* it."

Tory shook her head but said nothing.

The second floor had what Tory guessed were bedrooms, maybe a study or office or something (did they have those back in the 19th century?), and no signs of life.

At the far end of a hallway there was a small door that Rob tried, behind which they found one more flight of stairs. "The attics!" Rob whispered gleefully and led the way up. What they found was a narrow hall off which a series of closet-sized rooms opened. "This is where servants lived," Rob said.

"You mean slaves, right?" Tory corrected him. "I mean, why pay people when you can just own them and have them work for free?"

Rob gestured for her to follow him as he went into every one of the eight tiny rooms. Two had old, broken bedsteads in them, one a chest of drawers that squirrels had nested in. Rob put down his backpack on the floor of the last one on the left.

"This is the place," he said, his voice hushed and reverent.

"Why?"

"Because," Rob explained patiently as he unpacked his backpack, "all the articles and firsthand accounts and historical records say that the murder occurred in the servants' quarters," he was laying out food now, "and *that* it is most likely to be where the hauntings occur."

"Murder?!" Tory made no effort to whisper. "You didn't tell me the hauntings here were because of murder!"

"Most are," Rob said matter-of-factly, pulling open a bag of chips. "Ghosts always haunt for a reason, Tory—I've told you that before." He popped a couple of chips into his mouth, chewing loudly. "The most common reason is because of a violent death---it leaves them feeling unresolved, and that's why they come back." When Tory stayed standing up, arms folded, he went on. "It's not like they want revenge, it's more like they want to get back the time that was taken away from them. Don't worry---ghosts don't hurt you; they just haunt. There's nothing to be afraid of."

She exhaled an exasperated breath and pulled a Ziplock bag filled with an enormous slice of chocolate cake toward herself. "Whatever," was all she said before taking a bite.

"Even if this isn't the right room," Rob said after a few minutes of quiet munching, "when the supernatural visitor comes, we should be able to sense it up here, and go see where ever it is."

Tory merely rolled her eyes and took another bite of cake. She looked at her watch: 1:00 a.m. It was going to be a long night.

The sound of scrabbling and scratching from one of the other rooms got their attention. Rob jumped up, but Tory stayed where she was.

"It's probably just the squirrels from that nest in the dresser," she said.

"I'd better go see," Rob grabbed the flashlight and hurried out of the room. A few minutes later he was back, but without any light. "It was the squirrels," he said, sounding tense, "but the flashlight died. I just put new batteries in this afternoon!" He hit it against his palm a couple more times. "Would you get the candles out and light them?" Tory thought his voice shook slightly and wondered why he was so spooked all of a sudden. Wasn't this what he'd always wanted? Wasn't this a dream come true for him?

Out came the three pillar candles she'd brought, and soon the room was illuminated by their flickering, golden warmth.

Rob sat down and took the flashlight apart, checked the batteries, and put it back together again, but still couldn't make it work. He swore under his breath, then asked, "What time is it?"

"1:15."

Rob stood up and paced back and forth a few times. "I feel like we really need this to work," he said.

"We've got the candles," Tory pointed out. She couldn't understand why he was so upset about the flashlight.

"Tory, when I went down to that room, I felt…something," he crouched down in front of her and whispered. "There were squirrels, but there was something else too. I don't think we should be without some modern technology here."

"But you said that ghosts can upset batteries and lights and stuff," she exclaimed. "That's why I brought the candles! If they—or it—or whatever it is—already messed up your flashlight, then wouldn't anything else get messed up too?"

"I just don't feel right about it," Rob stood up again and paced some more. Suddenly he turned to face her. "Tell you what. There's still time, if I really push it, for me to go back, get some new batteries, and be here by 2:00. That's the witching hour, so I'd be in time, and I'll bring extra batteries and another flashlight too." He slapped his forehead with his palm. "Why I didn't think of that before, I don't know, but what do you say? Will you hold down the fort here for 45 minutes while I go get that stuff? Just to be extra safe?"

Tory couldn't believe it. "Rob, why take the chance on being seen or getting caught? Let's just stay put, keep the candles lit, and go home at 5:00 like we planned."

But Rob was shaking his head and already backing out of the room, reaching for his backpack as he moved. "I swear I'll go *super*-fast---I'll be back *before* 45 minutes. You'll see!"

And then she heard him running down the stairs. Two stories below her the wood of the front door protested with a loud creak. In the still night she could hear him dragging his bike through the tall grass, and then pedaling away.

"I don't believe this," Tory said in the silence that seemed to crowd into the room. She looked around. He'd left his bag of chips, and she decided it served him right if she finished it. The floor was hard and uncomfortable, so she stood and walked over to the small dormer window, bag of chips in hand, and looked out over the empty field below.

There was a hazy, thin light on the distant horizon, in the direction of town, where street lights and businesses, cars and porch lights banished the blackness of night. But all around her, the house, the field, the woods, shadows filled the landscape with mysterious depths, tricked the eye into seeing movement where all was still, black on grey on blue. She recognized the cry of an owl coming from the nearest stand of trees, but her eyes couldn't find its glowing eyes amid the skeletal branches. Tory leaned on the weathered window sill and peered toward the road, wondering how long she'd have to wait for Rob to get back.

Twenty-five minutes later the bag of chips was empty, and Tory was tired of waiting. She was starting to get angry. She turned from the window and walked the length of the room. This plan had better work, she fumed, to be worth a night without sleep, left alone in this forsaken place. After tonight, she *never* wanted to hear a single word about ghosts from him again.

Just then she heard something—not the scrabbling of squirrels, she was sure, something more definite-sounding. She went back to the window and looked over to where her bike was still resting beneath the tree. Rob's bike wasn't there, but she thought maybe he'd left it someplace else and was making his way upstairs already.

She waited, listening for his footsteps on the stairs.

There was nothing. Sdhe began to think she'd imagined it when suddenly she heard it again: a scraping sound, like metal on stone. It repeated twice more, then stopped.

Tory was puzzled, but only for a moment. "Robert Eugene Jones!" she said out loud, crumpling the chip bag and throwing it to the floor. "You are not going to fake-ghost your way out of this one!" She realized now that it was all a setup; he'd planned it from the start, the faulty batteries, the need to go for more, and now his own fake haunting, so she'd become a believer and jump on the Ghost Train with him.

Furious, she grabbed one of the candles and stomped out of the room, heading for the stairs. She glanced into each of the attic rooms as she stormed past them, but they were empty. He must be hiding somewhere down stairs.

When she emerged into the upstairs hallway she heard the sound again, closer—maybe coming from one of the rooms nearby? As she worked her way around the upstairs, looking inside room after room, she wondered what he was using to make that sound. She heard it again, now seeming to be outside the house altogether—a shovel? Was he dragging a shovel across something, maybe one of the old gravestones outside?

"Well that's not creepy," she said aloud, shivering a little. "Plus, disrespectful," she added, stoking her own anger at the lengths he was going to with this whole thing.

The sound came again, definitely outside this time.

"Enough is enough," Tory went into the nearest room and crossed to a window, all glass long gone from its sash, a gaping black hole opening out into the night. "Rob, I know it's you!" She shouted. "This isn't funny! I've had enough—I'm coming down to get my bike and go home!"

She listened for a response, maybe a giggle, anything that would give away where he was hiding, but heard nothing.

"If he knows what's good for him, he'll stay hidden," she muttered to herself as she turned from the window. Movement caught her eye. Holding the candle up, she expected to see Rob's grin somewhere in the gloom of the room behind her. It was still empty, but the door, which had been wide open and hanging at an odd angle, as if the top hinges were disconnected, was slowly swinging closed. There was not a breath of air in the room, no wind pushed through the dark window behind her, and yet the door moved.

When it reached the jamb it bumped softly, bounced back a few inches, and then seemed to try to close again, this time with slightly more force behind it.

Tory held her candle high above her head and squinted at the door. She couldn't see any strings attached, but decided that must be what he'd done, and he was on the other side, hidden in the shadows of the hall somewhere, pulling.

She moved toward the door slowly, thinking she might turn the tables on him by grabbing the door, pulling it open and jumping out at him. That'd teach him a lesson!

Just inches away from it, Tory lowered her candle to the same level as the door knob, looking for the string Rob was using. She couldn't see any. She was just about to reach out and grab the door to throw it open anyway, when she noticed something that made the hairs on the back of her neck rise up, and she gasped: the candle's flame was blue.

"Candles will burn with blue flame when ghosts are near," Rob had said. *"It's like an early warning system."*

The thumping of the door against its frame reminded Tory that there had to be an explanation—she needed to find the string tied to the other side, and no doubt there was some kind of powder or something he sprinkled on the candle before he left, when she wasn't looking, that would make this happen. With her heart beating a little faster now, she reached out for the door, caught its edge, and pushed it wide open.

There was no string on the door. She looked from top to bottom. She looked at the hinges. She felt along the top edge with her fingers. Nothing.

And her candle was still burning blue.

She jumped when another noise caught her attention. This was different. It sounded like it was coming from downstairs. Stepping carefully, Tory found her way to the main staircase and, gripping the banister, eyes searching the space ahead of her, she slowly descended. The blue flame burned without giving off much light, so she was feeling her way step by step, exploring each one with her toe before putting the whole weight of her foot down, all the time listening for Rob.

The sound came again—a clanking of metal, but this time sounding more like pots being jumbled together, or maybe metal tools in a tool box rattling around. She followed it to the back of the house, a room she and Rob had figured was the kitchen when they'd explored earlier. Two of the four walls were filled with large windows, free of glass but wooden frames in place, and Tory had the uncomfortable feeling that instead of letting in light, they were filled with inky blackness, shadows rising from beneath the trees and dark places outside, pushing in and filling the room.

She shivered and realized that it was so cold she could see her breath pluming out in front of her. Cold like this usually didn't arrive in southeastern Virginia until well into January, but Tory was sure that if the windows had had any glass left in them, she'd see a filigree of frost curling over their surface.

The noise sounded again, behind her. She turned and saw that there was a closed door—somehow they'd missed it earlier, or she was sure Rob would've insisted they check it out. Or was that his plan all along? Filling her lungs with the frigid air, Tory crossed to the door, placed her hand on the nob, and turned it.

The metal was so cold it burned her palm, but the door swung open easily, only the merest sigh from the old hinges. Holding the candle high again, vainly hoping for illumination from the cold, blue flame, she stepped down into the darkness.

The metallic sound was coming from whatever place was beneath the kitchen, at the bottom of the stairs. Slowly, step by step, Tory descended, straining her eyes to see what it was—Rob? An old furnace trying to come to life? An animal? She felt compelled to follow it, to find its source, to understand.

At the bottom of the stairs she stood still and listened. For a few moments there was silence, and then, louder and closer than before, she heard it—and with it came a strong wind, smelling of dirt and rocks and rotting wood, and out went the candle.

The darkness around her was complete. No light penetrated from the kitchen above, although she was sure the door was still open. The air felt thick and stirred with invisible motion nearby. A heavy, rasping breath whispered something from across the space in front of her, but she could not understand the words, only feel the disturbance it caused brush against her cheek.

Rob?

She wanted to call his name, tell him it was time to stop, this was going too far, but found that she couldn't move—not her feet, not her hands, not her mouth; she was frozen with terror, unable to break free.

The voice murmured again, ending with an evil chuckle, and across the room Tory could see something moving. Slowly it became clear, the darkness fading to grey around a hunched shape, like an old man, carrying something on his back. His muttering grew louder, and he slung the bag from his shoulder to the dirt floor with a wet thud. Tory didn't want to think about what might be in that bag but couldn't tear her eyes away.

Next, he reached down to pick up an object, which he began to thrust into the ground. It was a shovel, by the sound of it, and it made that same grating, metal on stone sound she'd heard upstairs in the attic room. Time seemed frozen. Tory had no sense of how long she stood there, witnessing his toil, hearing his oily aspirations and smug, wicked laughter. Finally, he dropped the shovel—*that's the clattering I heard from the stairs,* she realized, as she watched him turn and begin to rummage with the bag, trying to open it and take something out.

I don't want to see this, I don't want to see this, Tory screamed silently inside her head, but no amount of trying closed her eyelids, nothing she could do would break her feet free and take her back up the stairs.

The wretch was making angry noises of frustration when suddenly he looked up, across the bag, across the room, and saw her. No scream was possible, and Tory thought her heart would give out it was pounding so fast. He paused, his eyes locked onto hers, and then, dropping the bag, he began to creep toward her.

Tory watched his lurching, hunched form getting closer. His eyes glinted with the phosphorescence of rotten flesh and his gaze bored into her. She knew that if he reached her, she would never leave that basement.

Only a few feet away, a toothless, beastly grin smeared across his face, the figure suddenly froze, turning its head as if listening. Tory held her breath. She heard footsteps in the kitchen, on the stairs behind her.

"Tory? What--!"

The monstrous shadow creature leaned forward once more, then, throwing up an arm as if to ward off a blow, gave a guttural cry of pain and fell backward.

Suddenly Tory found she could turn her head. As she did, she heard the distant crowing of a rooster. She looked up the stairs and saw Rob a few stairs above, a look of shock on his face. He was outlined by the faint light of dawn beginning to bloom across the top of the wall. Without waiting another second, she threw the candle down and ran up the stairs through the house, out the front door to where her bike lay waiting.

Rob was close on her heels.

"Tory? What *was* that? What *happened?*"

She didn't stop to explain. She jumped on her bike and pedaled as hard as she could, Rob panting behind her, trying to keep up. Halfway home she realized she'd left her backpack on the floor of the attic room, but didn't even consider going back for it.

She'd been wanting a new one, anyway.

"Can U come over?" Rob texted around noon.

Tory texted back a thumbs up and headed down the block to his house.

"Sorry about last night," They were sitting in Rob's room, just like usual. Rob kicked the rug with the toe of his sneakers and didn't look her in the eye.

"What took you so long?" was all she could think of to say.

"My bike got a flat tire." But he still wasn't looking at her, so Tory didn't buy it.

Maybe, after all his talk, he just chickened out.

"So, did you see anything?" He asked. "I mean, things seemed…weird…when I got there…"

"I ate all your chips. And finished the cake, too. By the time you got there I wasn't feeling too good."

"Ha," he chuckled, and then hesitantly repeated, "Did you *see* anything?"

Tory felt the hairs rise on the back of her neck. Instead of answering his question, she asked, "What did you see? When you got there, I mean. Did *you* see anything?"

Rob frowned. "I couldn't see much. It looked like your candle went out down there and—was there something moving around? An animal or…something?" Did he sound hopeful, or worried? She couldn't quite tell.

"I'm not sure what I saw," she looked away.

"Huh," Rob sounded disappointed. "Well, maybe you'll remember something…later." He half smiled at her. "Sorry if I wasted your time. I really thought—all the stuff I read said it's a real haunted house."

"Forget it," Tory said quickly. "Seriously. Listen, have you done the English homework yet? There are a lot of questions on the reading this time."

"Not yet. Want to work on it together?"

"Sure."

The homework took two hours. When they finally finished Tory stretched, yawning.

"I'm done. Think I'll go home and call it an early night."

"Wait, let me get you some of the cookies mom baked yesterday— they're really good," and before she could object, he ran out of the room and down the stairs to the kitchen.

While she waited, Tory looked at her friend's bookshelves. All those books about ghosts, haunted places, supernatural phenomena…she wandered over for a closer look at some of the titles. One in particular caught her attention: "True Ghost Stories," by Helmer O. Wattenford.

She was halfway through the summary on the back cover when she heard Rob's feet pounding up the stairs.

"Here you go!" Rob grinned, handing her a bag that must have held a dozen cookies. She guessed his guilt over last night was the reason for this bounty. Plus, he knew her passion for chocolate chips.

"Are you sure your mom won't miss this many?"

"She can bake more."

"Okay, thanks. Mind if I borrow this?" She held the book out for him to see. His eyebrows went up in surprise, and she shrugged as if it wasn't very important. "I was just thinking, maybe it would help me remember what I saw...or something."

"Sure!" He grinned, and she put it into her backpack.

He walked her down to the front door. "See you tomorrow at school?"

"Yup," Tory said, over her shoulder as she walked down the front stairs to the sidewalk. "See you tomorrow."

She wasn't really all that tired. The second her head hit the pillow she'd fallen asleep, and her mom had let her sleep in until 11:00. She planned to go home, stash the bag of cookies in the pantry, then go to her room and check out the book she'd borrowed.

Maybe she'd been a little too hard on Rob. Maybe there was something to all this ghost stuff after all.

2

BONFIRE

It had always been Siobhan's job.

With her harelip and ice-blue eyes, she seemed marked from birth to be Gran's apprentice and, eventually, to take her place. From the time she was big enough to carry the basket of food, Siobhan was sent from the cluster of houses in the valley, across the windy pastures, to ascend the foothills and climb the rocky path that led to the ancient standing stones where Gran built the bonfire every year on the Longest Night. And it was Siobhan who, just before dawn, returned the way she had come, carrying a large turnip filled with live coals which would kindle the hearth fires of every family in the village, new light in the first dark days of the new year.

But Siobhan couldn't go this year. Taken by a sickness that not even Gran's herbs could cure, she lay buried with the ancestors, sleeping in the cold ground.

It fell to Aisling now. She was only 8, and the idea of walking alone through the dark to Gran, and walking home before dawn, terrified her. Secretly, when she was supposed to be gathering wood or carding wool or filling the water buckets in the stream, Aisling stole away to walk the path by daylight---or as much of it as time allowed—hoping to memorize the way enough to avoid catastrophe.

But at night she dreamed of wandering in a desolate place, nothing familiar, no one hearing her cries for help. Sometimes she found herself plummeting off a slippery stone into an abyss, only to wake, her heart beating wildly, before she hit the bottom. Other nights she struggled against the tarry sucking of a peat bog pulling her slowly down, and woke gasping for air, clawing at the bed, desperate to get away. Whatever the dream, she was alone, always alone, no one to help, no one to see her.

"Is it demons you're afraid of?" Seamus, her older brother, asked when she'd awakened him yet again with her nightmare cries. "Bogeymen and Banshees and such?" Seamus loved telling stories of the dark ends of weary travelers, waylaid and overcome by any number of shadowy, evil creatures that populated his imagination. Often enough his tales sent the younger children crying to their mother's skirts, and Da would give Seamus an extra hour of chores as punishment for frightening them.

Aisling had never been troubled by them, however. Pushing her hair away from her sweaty brow, she shook her head. "Not a bit of it," she said stubbornly. "Siobhan never said she saw such things, on all the nights she walked to Gran's. I don't believe in your bogeymen and banshees."

"Well," Seamus yawned, rolling over and burrowing under the blanket they shared, "if you're not afraid of that, then I'd say you've nothing to fear. Go to sleep, will you?"

But sleep had left her for the night, and as soon as dawn crept into the windows, she wrapped herself warmly and snuck away to walk the path again, determined to learn it as well as she could before Longest Night, trying to push away the terror of walking unaccompanied through the wilderness of darkness she knew awaited her.

But walking it at dawn, or midday, or in the purple dusk was different altogether from walking it in the black of night, and when she found herself at last facing the trek, her confidence fled and fear walked with her. Every pebble, every hillock, every wind-stunted tree seemed unfamiliar. She second-guessed every turn, backtracked, and repeated her steps so often that the distance she walked tripled what it should have been.

She was supposed to be to Gran well before midnight, but Aisling could tell by the moon that midnight was near, and she had a long way to go, "If I get there at all," she thought mournfully. She stopped beside a boulder which she thought she recognized, finding it a comfort to see something that was even slightly familiar, and sat on it to rest for a few moments. She gazed up at the stars, and thought suddenly that if she'd been cleverer, she would have asked old MacDougal to teach her to read the stars for direction and used them to guide her at night. Shaking her head at her own stupidity, she heaved a deep sigh.

"It sounds like a heavy burden weighs upon you," the words growled out from the shadows behind her. "A sigh like that is much too dark and sad for one so small as you."

Aisling jumped off the boulder and turned to face the voice. At first all she could see was a shadowy form, something chiseled out of the night itself. But it moved forward, and she realized it was a large man wearing a black cloak, standing just behind her boulder. He seemed made of darkness: dark hair, long and freely hanging around his shoulders, dark eyes whose color she could not see, a dark complexion, which she thought odd for this time of year when hours of sunlight were so few.

"Good evening," she found her voice saying, and felt a little wonder that she could remember manners on such a night, in such a place.

"Is it?" The stranger nodded at her in a friendly way. "I'm glad to hear you say so. For you sounded, a moment ago, as if perhaps it was not."

"I have a long walk ahead of me, and the night is dark, and I am afraid of getting lost," Aisling explained frankly. She saw no reason not to be honest, her mother had taught her to respect her elders and be truthful always.

"Perhaps some company along your way would shorten the distance and lighten your heart?" the stranger bowed low and smiled.

"I would welcome it!" she exclaimed, relief lightening her heart. She felt her back straighten as the weight of her fears began to leave her.

"Then by all means, let us walk together." The stranger came around from behind the boulder, and together they continued along the way that led to Gran's. After a few moments of companionable silence, the stranger asked, "May I ask the name of the young lady with whom I walk?"

Aisling chuckled at the formality of his request and answered him. "Aisling. I come from the village down in the glen." She peered up at the stranger's face, but the hood of his cloak hid most of it from her. "What is your name, sir?"

"You may call me Billy, though I have other names as well."

They lapsed into another silence. Aisling felt a growing confidence that she was following the same path she'd rehearsed so many times. Having Billy beside her bolstered her mood. She began to sing a tune she'd heard Siobhan sing, and when she'd finished Billy complimented her.

"I've heard that before, but never sung by so sweet a voice," he smiled down at her, and she could see his teeth glinting in the moonlight. "Tell me, young Aisling, are you not afraid to walk on the Longest Night, alone? I see you have a basket, and must be bringing something to someone, but why not wait 'til morning?"

Aisling explained as she carefully chose her steps across the boggy field they had come to. "It is my task to bring provisions to my Gran, who waits at the Standing Stones on the mountain top, where she will kindle the Bonfire this Longest Night. There I will sit with her as she invokes the spirits' good will for a blessed and bountiful year, and when she is done it is my task to return to the village with coals from the fire to rekindle every hearth. They've all been put out as the sun set tonight, and the village waits in darkness for new light, which will carry the blessings of the spirits, and see us into the new year." She paused to carefully consider her next step, saw a stunted tree that she recognized, and chose her footing with confidence. "My sister Siobhan used to do this. Everyone thought she was touched by the Sidhs, so that she would take Gran's place. But she died at harvest time, and there is no one but me to do it now."

"No one?" Billy sounded surprised. "But surely there are others in your village who could do this."

Aisling considered a moment before answering. She did not wish to be deceitful, and knew she had nothing to be ashamed of, but some things felt like the things one should hold close. "The elders chose me. Gran agreed with them. And so here I am," was what she settled on saying.

Billy nodded as if he understood more than she'd said.

"But surely such a night as this holds terror for you?" Billy prodded her a bit with his words, and she frowned, wondering what he was getting at. "Have you not heard stories of the Lair Bhan, the ghastly white horse that gallops across the moors auguring death? Such a night as this, when darkness is king and the Other World is close by, the Lair Bhan may be seen." He rubbed his hands together, and Aisling could hear the rasping of his skin, as if it were calloused and rough.

"Certainly," she answered carefully, "everyone knows this. But death comes to all, and seeing the Lair Bhan only gives you warning, it's not a curse itself." She didn't tell him that Siobhan had seen the wraith herself, late last summer, and told her of it, warning that her time was near.

The wind picked up, and it almost sounded like the distant galloping of a horse, but the sound disappeared as soon as she listened for it, and Billy was talking again.

"Then what about Lady Gwynn, the headless maiden, and her black boar, who chase luckless wanderers like yourself?" Billy seemed to chuckle as he said this, and Aisling wondered why.

"In all the tales I've heard told, as the firelight dies and darkness gathers in the corners," she said quietly, "No one in our village has ever claimed to see Lady Gwynn, though I have of course heard her story. I think she must roam elsewhere, and so she is no concern of mine."

They walked in silence for a time. Aisling noted with satisfaction that the ground was rising, growing drier and rockier. She had reached the foothills, the final stretch of her journey. The moon, though less than half full, was high in the sky and its light told her that midnight had passed. She moved her feet faster, beginning to worry that Gran would be cross with her when she arrived so late.

"You can't expect me to believe," Billy spoke again, "that you don't fear the Sluagh, soul hunters from the West, out to steal souls for their Dark Master on dark nights when the shadows are thick, and the sun is long hours away."

Panting slightly from the exertion of moving faster and going uphill, Aisling smiled because she recognized the path that would take her the last leg of the journey to her Gran, and over her shoulder she said, "But the moon is bright tonight, and I see the way clearly. I hear no hunting cries. Why should I fear such creatures? Surely, they are more the stuff of ghost stories meant to frighten my little brothers and sisters, than true figments of this world, and pose no real danger? "

The wind cried out as it coursed over the rocky mountainside, and Aisling at last could see the silhouettes of the Standing Stones where Gran was waiting. The flickering light of a great bonfire leapt up into the star-filled sky, and she paused to catch her breath.

"Sir, your company has been a great comfort to me, and I am sure you'd be welcomed by Gran if you care to—" Aisling gaped at the empty path behind her, straining her eyes for Billy somewhere in the landscape of stone and shadows.

But he was nowhere to be seen.

Was that burnt smell from the bonfire? Is that why her mouth suddenly had the taste of bitter ashes?

A shiver ran through her body, and Aisling hurried the rest of the way to Gran. The old woman clasped her in a tight embrace, and then took her shoulders in her hands and gave her a shake.

"What is it's been keeping you this long time?" She demanded, fear and relief mingling in her voice.

Aisling told her about the long walk through the dark, her fear of getting lost, and Billy, while unpacking the basket and helping to bring another armload of fuel for the bonfire. Her gran listened silently, then motioned for her to follow, leading her to a place before the great fire where there was a log to sit on, and a smooth place cleared in the dirt.

From a sack she pulled stones, feathers, powders, and a flask of liquid that smelled of pine trees and star light. She watched as her gran placed each thing carefully before the fire in the cleared space, listened as she sang a song with words Aisling had never heard before, and did not recognize. She gasped when she saw her gran rub the fragrant liquid over her hands, and then reach over, into the heart of the fire, drawing out a long stick, glowing with heat and smoking as it burned, yet did not burn her. With the stick she drew patterns in the soft dirt around the stones and things she'd placed there, and a haze seemed to rise around them which made Aisling imagine she could see the night air around them like a fog, swirling and billowing, and then parting like a curtain outside the ring of light.

She saw the symbols dance with the rocks, undulating to the rhythm of her gran's song, and the feathers multiplied themselves until they filled the sky and floated away to the moon. She heard sounds in the night, and peering through the curtain of darkness, she saw eyes in strange faces, shapes of creatures unlike any she knew. A pageant of pale, wailing figures emerged from the depth of the shadows about them: a troop of hunters with pointed ears and wicked faces, hallooing and galloping on strange, headless horses in pursuit of their quarry; a small group of lurching, hump-backed, three-legged brown things with faces like crying babies, who she knew wanted only what they did not possess and would do anything to get it for themselves; a magnificent yet terrible white horse with blood-red eyes and hooves galloped past, pausing to rear up and scream as only horses can, before disappearing again; a misty figure which seemed only halfway there, drawing nearer in a slow, meandering way as if lost and wandering, which Aisling saw presently was a slim maiden dressed in a gown of moonlight, who had no head above her shoulders, and she carried in her arms a black pig which wheezed and squealed and struggled but never escaped her grasp; behind her there thundered a host of headless riders, galloping on steeds with eyes of flame and pelts of tar; and at last, at the end of the procession, a tall figure in a cloak whose step Aisling felt was familiar, though when she squinted through the smoke and sparks to get a clearer view of it, she thought she spied a pair of hooves peeking out from beneath the long cloak, and a lock of dark hair escaping the hood before this figure, too, melted into the night.

In wonder and awe Aisling turned to her gran.

"Did you see that?" she asked.

Her gran nodded gravely. "I did. They come every Longest Night, the Dark Ones, from the deepest reaches of hell and nightmare, and walk the earth." She nodded toward the bonfire, now beginning to die down, and as she spoke Aisling noticed that a small wind was blowing from the sea now, and the stars had dimmed a little. "This fire is our protection from them, and these spells," she pointed to the stones and feathers and drawings in the dirt, which now looked like little more than a child's playthings, carelessly left behind when supper is called, "help us sustain its protection throughout the year."

Aisling's eyes were wide. "Do you mean that all the ghost stories and tales of demons that Seamus always tells are true?"

Gran chuckled. "Perhaps not Seamus's stories exactly," she allowed, "but evil is real, and there are dark things worth fearing."

"The Lair Bhan and Lady Gwyn? The sluagh and dullahan?"

"And even the Devil himself, who wanders the world looking for those he can trick through fear to strike deals which, in the end, will make their souls his, when he comes to claim them. Yes, even he."

Aisling shivered as the wind picked up. She recognized it as the first stirrings of a new day.

Gran fed her a warmed oatcake, gave her hot tea to wash it down, and as the edge of the sky began to green with the coming dawn she sent Aisling down the path, back to the village in the glen, carrying a basket containing a hollowed-out turnip—the biggest Aisling had ever seen—glowing with coals taken from the heart of the bonfire, ready to begin the hearth fires of her friends and neighbors, sustaining them all with warmth and protection for the year to come.

The walk home seemed much shorter. Aisling was full of wonder at the things she'd seen, and what she'd guessed about her companion from the night before. When she questioned her gran about Billy, she said, "You were never in danger, as your fear was already cured by his company. He couldn't spook you and trick you into anything, because of himself."

She wondered if Siobhan had ever walked beside Billy, in all the years she was sent to bring the coals back. As she rounded the last hill, a dewy light touched the stones of the first wall marking the valley she called home. Something made her stop and turn. Peering into a stand of trees, she thought she saw movement—something white, translucent, flitting between the trunks. Then the faintest sound of song, a whisp of tune, a fleeting hint of melody sung by a familiar voice.

Aisling smiled as she took the last steps toward home. She feared no evil. In the pearly light of dawn, she felt the stuff of time and the world thrumming around her, and part of it was her sister, and the spells Gran had woven, and even though the shadows were there too, she knew they could not touch her.

3

THE HANGING TREE

Jonathan sat back on his heels and blew out his breath in frustration. Mama had been the one with the magic touch when it came to lighting fires. She could make that smoke curl up with nothing but a few dry leaves, a twig, and some grass. She'd tried to teach him, but he just didn't have the knack for it.

You'll get it soon enough, she had promised him. *Just keep practicing.*

A cold wind stirred the branches of the ancient, gnarled oak above him, and he squinted at the setting sun. He was going to need the warmth of a fire tonight.

He hunched back over his small pile of twigs and grasses and started rubbing the stick back and forth between his palms, trying to ignore the blisters he could feeling coming up.

"You might try pulling that wad of grass back, son," a voice behind him said. "Let your wood breathe a bit, so it can start to burn."

Jonathan jumped at the sound, dropping his stick. He looked over his shoulder and saw the silhouette of a short, fat man standing a few feet behind him. He knew he should stand up to show respect, but he was hungry and tired and instead he just stared at him, silent.

"Ah," he said after a few moments had passed, "allow me to introduce myself. I am Horace Watford. I travel around these parts buying and selling and generally providing the brave souls who've settled out here with entertaining exotica to brighten their otherwise workaday lives." He spoke like someone reciting lines in a play, Jonathan thought, though he'd only seen one play, and that when he was only seven years old, and the family had gone to Sacramento. It was the only time he'd ever traveled so far or spent so much time off the farm. Until now.

"I'm Jonathan," he said quietly, still crouched over his pile of sticks and dry grass.

"Jonathan my boy, pleased to meet you!" Horace Watford exclaimed, and in three strides was standing over him, beaming. "I see you are attempting to bring light and warmth to your camp on this cold evening." He, too, hunkered down and peered at what Jonathan had collected and arranged for the purposes of fire making. "While my fingers are not as nimble as yours, perhaps I may be of service in offering advice for getting things started?"

Jonathan wasn't sure if the man was making fun of him, talking the way he did: too many words, too formal. What adult talked to a twelve-year-old boy that way? But he could feel it getting colder, so he nodded agreement.

"Ah, yes," Horace rubbed his hands together vigorously. "Now if you'll push back that wad of grass, my lad, and resume your frictional stick spinning, I believe—ah!" He drew in his breath and sat back on his heels. "There you have it!"

Smoke was twisting up from the small pieces of wood, and Jonathan grinned as he fed the dry grass to the little spark, watching it grow until he could add larger wood chips and, eventually, some of the larger pieces he'd gathered.

Horace Watford watched him work, a benevolent smile wreathing his round face. When the fire was sturdy enough for Jonathan to sit back on his heels and let it burn, Horace fixed him with a stern look and said, "My boy, you appear to be on your own out here."

"Yes sir." Jonathan looked away for a moment, then back into his fire.

"I see." The older man sucked on his bottom lip for a moment. "Well, as we find ourselves in a similar solitary predicament, I believe our wisest course would be to join forces and provide each other with camaraderie for a time."

Jonathan wrinkled his brow and squinted at Horace. "Sir?"

"Why not set up camp together is what I'm saying!" Horace bellowed a laugh that made Jonathan smile, in spite of the oddness of the man and his discomfort with strangers. As if he could read his mind, he continued, "After sharing a camp fire, no two people can remain strangers---'prairie kin' I've heard it called, the bond that forms in such situations." He lowered himself into a comfortable position across from Jonathan and gestured for Jonathan to do the same.

Horace Watford had spun tales of his travels and the strange and wondrous things he'd seen for nearly an hour before the sound of Jonathan's stomach rumbling interrupted.

"That is my cue, I believe, to suggest we pause to dine," he said with a slight incline of his head.

"Sir?"

Horace smiled patiently. "Have you any supper with you?"

Jonathan's face fell into a quiet kind of misery. "Only some jerky. I et all the rest, sir. It's the last I've got." He turned away and rummaged through a sack stowed safely away from the fire, turning back with a handful of stringy meat that looked tough enough to stand in for rope, should the need arise.

"Alas," Horace placed a hand on his chest and rolled his eyes to the starry sky dramatically, "jerked beef upsets my constitution with a greater ferocity than I can tolerate." He sighed deeply, then looked at his young companion and winked. "Go ahead and finish it yourself, my boy. I have," he chuckled and slapped his belly, "plenty stored up for nights like this."

Not wishing to be disrespectful, but relieved all the same, Jonathan smiled and began to eat the last of his dried beef.

As he gnawed at the meager dinner, the peddler continued his talking, sometimes reminiscing of his own childhood, often speculating and commenting on matters that Jonathan could not comprehend but supposed had to do with a world in which well-traveled men with money and education would feel at home. Jonathan found himself able to forget, for a time, that he was alone in the world, that this was the last of his food, that he didn't know how much further it was to the next town or if he'd find any work there. Horace talked so much that Jonathan didn't think even one time of the three graves he'd had to dig, or the wretched sickness that had preceded his doing so. The sound of flies buzzing in the hot afternoon sunshine, the smell of unwashed bedding, the hopelessness of releasing the livestock so they could forage for themselves—none of it returned to him that night as he scooted closer to the fire, listening to Mr. Watford's stories. As his eyelids grew heavy, the last, glassy look of his baby sister's gaze, lifeless, meaningless, desolate, did not float behind them, nor torment his dreams.

He awoke because it was light, well past dawn, and the last embers of his fire were no longer enough to keep the chill off. For just a moment he couldn't remember where he was, and he wondered why Mama hadn't woken him earlier to go milk the cow.

With shuddering force, it all came back. He gasped and sat up, looking around.

Mr. Horace Watford was gone, not a trace of him anywhere, not even foot prints leading away from the dusty fireside where they'd camped all night.

Shivering—from memory, from cold, from hunger—Jonathan rose, kicked dirt over the last of the fire's coals, hefted his sack, and set out on his westward path toward hope.

He saw the buildings on the horizon after only an hour of walking and quickened his pace. By noon he was walking down the main street, passing men and women on horses, a wagon. He could see people inside buildings, through the windows of various businesses. He recalled that Mr. Watford had advised him to stop in at the general store and ask there if they mightn't need an extra hand. He'd said that the man who ran it was kind and would help him find work if he didn't need the help himself. Jonathan saw the sign at the far end of the main street,

"Goodman's General Store." Hoping that the name was a good sign, he mounted the steps and opened the door.

Inside it was quiet and warm. There were two customers walking among the goods, and one at the counter being helped by a man with long whiskers and bright eyes.

"You bring it right back here if it doesn't meet your needs, Mrs. Wells," he said. "I'll find you something that will do what you need, one way or the other."

"Thank you, Mr. Goodman," the woman took a package wrapped in brown paper from the counter and tucked it under her arm. "Please give my best to Mrs. Goodman."

They nodded at each other, and she left. There was the tinkle of a little bell when she opened the door, and Jonathan smiled when he heard it. It reminded him of a bell they'd had at home, one Mama kept in a special place on the mantel over the fireplace, and she'd ring it on special days—Christmas, Easter, birthdays—and tell the story of how it was brought over by her grandfather from the old country.

The smile faded from his face and the joy fell away from him as fast as the memory came, and it was his quiet grief that got Mr. Goodman's attention.

"Can I help you, son?" He was leaning across the counter top, peering at Jonathan with a kindness that nearly made him unable to answer.

"Yes sir. I'm looking for work, sir," he stared down at his shoes as he spoke to avoid seeing the gentleness that made him feel he might fall apart right there, in front of strangers, in a public place.

"Work?" The man stood up straight and folded his arms. "Shouldn't you be in school?"

Jonathan shook his head from side to side. "I'm from yonder," he waved eastward, toward the open lands he'd traversed alone, back toward the abandoned farm and the three lonely graves, the flies, the empty barn, and the past. "I've got to find my way now, sir," was all he could think of to explain his situation.

"I see," Mr. Goodman stroked his beard thoughtfully. "Why'd you stop in here? Have you shop work experience?"

"No sir," Jonathan shook his head again. "But I was advised by a Mr. Watford that you might have a job for someone like myself." He looked up hopefully. "And if not, you might be able to help me find work someplace else."

The pale and staring countenance of Mr. Goodman made Jonathan think he'd offended him, and he quickly continued. "I'm sorry to have troubled you, sir." He took three steps toward the door and began to reach for the handle.

Mr. Goodman was there first. "You're not going anywhere, son," he said in a quiet, but not angry, voice. Jonathan looked up at him. "I perceive that you have been on the road a while and could use a place to rest and gather yourself together." He nodded toward the back corner of the room. "In the back I have a small closet with a cot. You'd be welcome to stop there for a while. As it happens, I expect a large shipment tomorrow, and could use some help with it. In return, I'll see that you're fed, and the cot is yours as long as you stay on." He squinted down at Jonathan and put a hand on his shoulder. "Will this arrangement suit you?"

Jonathan felt his legs go weak with relief. "Yes sir," he stuttered. "It's very good of you sir." He followed Mr. Goodman across the large store and back to the door in the corner, behind which was a short hallway that ended in a kind of large storage closet, where indeed there was a cot. "Mr. Watford said you were kind to young folk, sir, and I'm grateful."

Mr. Goodman stood in the doorway of the closet and silently watched Jonathan place his bag under the bed. "Where did you meet Mr. Watford?" He asked.

"It was last night," Jonathan told him, sitting on the cot, and feeling more tired than he could ever remember feeling, even after the long days helping Papa during spring planting, or that time when a blizzard snowed them in, and they had to spend hours digging a tunnel to the barn so they could reach the livestock. Papa had been so angry because he said there weren't supposed to be blizzards in California.

"Near here?" Mr. Goodman prompted the boy gently.

"Half a day's walk. I stopped for the night under a great big oak tree, and he found me there, helped me with my campfire and stayed for the night."

Mr. Goodman nodded gravely, his eyes unfocused, his mouth frowning slightly. Then he shook his head and smiled down at Jonathan.

"You take a little rest after your long walk, son, then come on out and I'll show you how things work in the store. We'll have supper at 6:00. My wife will welcome a fresh face at the table."

Jonathan lay back gratefully on the cot, falling asleep even as his head touched the soft pallet.

Mr. Goodman left the door ajar and returned to his front counter, where two people were waiting. The first bought a few items, paid, and left swiftly. The second was Francois DuTot, an old friend of John Goodman's.

"Did I hear that boy say that Watford sent him?" DuTot leaned close to his old friend.

"You did."

"Do you think it was *our* Watford?"

John Goodman looked levelly at him. "What else am I to think?" He said after a silence.

DuTot whistled a long, low whistle and shook his head. "This is what, the third time?"

"Fourth by my count."

"Why does he do it?" DuTot asked loudly enough that Goodman gestured for him to hush. "Why do you suppose he don't just stay dead?"

"That's more than I can try to answer," said John Goodman. He told Francois DuTot how much he owed for the hammer and nails and bag of flour he'd come for, accepted his money, and wished him good day.

He knew that DuTot would go to the saloon that night and spread word that the peddler's ghost had struck again. They'd tell and retell the story of how the peddler had come to town ten years ago, right about the time a local man's family had been murdered in their sleep. He came screaming into town, crying that they'd been attacked, blood on his clothes. He said it was the peddler, trying to rob them while they slept, who'd done it. As the man was a local and the peddler was not, judgement went against him, and he was hung outside of town, though he protested his innocence to the last.

John had not been comfortable with it at the time and was even less so when the man whose family had been killed was caught trying to rob another family nearby, threatening them at knifepoint, only six months later. It was sheer luck that the eldest boy had been visiting the outhouse when this evil man entered. He was able to surprise him from behind, knock the knife out of his hand, and save his family. The would-be thief got away and no one ever saw him again, but the same could not be said for the innocent peddler who'd been hung for another man's crimes.

Every now and then a stranger would come into town, and it'd come out that he'd seen the peddler—always near the hanging tree. Once a young child whose family was new to the community had wandered off and gotten lost. The parents and able-bodied adults of the town searched three days and nights for him with no result; but on the fourth day he toddled back into town, and in his childish way he explained that he'd been playing with a fat man who sold things, and it was he who told him to go back home and showed him the way.

John Goodman believed that the peddler wanted to prove to the townsfolk that he had been innocent and was doing it by helping folks when he could. He especially seemed to want to aid the young, and John remembered with some discomfort the sickened shock on the peddler's face when he'd been accused of viciously murdering those children.

But there was no sense discussing it with Francois. He was a good man and a good friend, but also something of a gossip. Let him go and sift through it all with the others who liked to drink and speculate about such things, and then go and spin tall tales about them. John Goodman would take care of this boy. It was a hard life, and this could be a hard country. If the peddler sent the boy to him there must be a reason. Whether or not he understood them, John intended to honor the wishes of the ghost of Horace Watford.

4
———

VAMPYRE

**Mysteries of Washington
High**

*By Roxanne Chance, Investiga-
tive Reporter*

We've all heard the stories.

…There's a ghost in the auditorium that always appears on
opening night of the spring play.

…Sometimes the janitors
hear strange sounds late at
night, and there's a rumor that
a woman who bears a striking
resemblance to the school nurse
back in 1958 occasionally is seen
walking down the dark hallways
in her sensible shoes.

…There's been talk of teachers having to avoid the second-
floor lounge, because from time

to time it fills with smoke from an unidentified source, and someone once heard ghastly coughing coming from the room, when no one was there.

…There are locker room stories too, like the one about the cheer leader and her quarterback boyfriend who were murdered by a mysterious, shadowy figure while having a tryst in the girls' showers, back in the '70's.

…And every one of us knows the legend about the phantom band that some kids a few years ago swore they saw marching across the football field after the Homecoming Dance—although it *was* foggy, and their relative states of sobriety have good reason to be questioned.

Fellow Washingtonians, why is our school the subject of so many strange tales? Is there any truth to the story that the school was built on top of an old settler cemetery, making it a prime location for supernatural phenomena? Are the lei lines that so many of the more hippy-inclined members of the community love to talk about, somehow real and responsible? Could there be a scientific, otherworldly explana-

tion, such as Senior Class Pres-
ident Preston Wild proposed
with his now legendary tweet
about aliens creating these "effects," making our school their
laboratory in order to see how
we young people of earth might
respond?

It's time we had a proper investigation of our history, and
someone to delve into each of the
outrageous legends and myths
concerning our school. We have
a right to know the truth of the
matter, whether we are at risk,
and what, if anything, needs to
be done!

This column will be a weekly
investigation into the stories,
myths, sightings, and historic
background of our school community. We welcome any tips
or eye-witness reports, and authentic, verifiable photos and
video footage will be featured
prominently.

Bring us your stories, and
we'll get to the bottom of them!

Gabby sat back and sighed with satisfaction. She had always dreamed
of being an investigative journalist. No freshmen were allowed to
enroll in journalism, but she made sure it was at the top of her course
list, her first elective choice for her sophomore year, and now—at last!
—she had the chance to fulfill her dream.

"'Roxanne'?" Ms. Bloom, the journalism teacher, looked at her with amusement. "Most journalists don't use a *nom de plume*, you know."

"It's my middle name," Gabby explained, "and I've always wanted to use it for professional purposes."

"I see. Well," Ms. Bloom hesitated as she finished reading the article over Gabby's shoulder, "we've never had anyone take on a weekly column like this before." She glanced down at Gabby, putting one hand on her hip. "Do you mean this seriously? Or is this meant to be a series of humor pieces?"

"Humor?" Gabby jumped up from her chair, surprising Ms. Bloom and catching the attention of several other students in the class. "Not at all! This is serious investigative journalism, Ms. B! I mean, come on," she pointed down at the computer screen, "just like I said in the article, we've all heard all the crazy, spooky stories forever, and so did our parents when they went here, but no one has ever looked into it!" She looked around at the kids who were staring, and a couple of them nodded. "We should find out what we can and tell everyone—the public has a right to know!"

A few students smirked, but several seemed to appreciate her enthusiasm and her idea. Ms. Bloom said, "All right, if it's your passion, by all means, pursue it. But tread carefully when you investigate—especially if you're talking about going into that 2nd floor lounge," and she made a face that several kids laughed at as she went back to her desk.

Within hours of her story going live on the school's news website, Gabby received three anonymous tips. By the end of the school day there were five.

"How do people leave anonymous tips for you?" her friend Lesley asked, when she told her about it after school. "The comments section under your article requires a name and email."

"Yeah, but people can click on my name and go to my staff page, and send me emails that way," Gabby hugged her books to her chest as she walked. "I only had time to glance at them, but I think some are jokes. Anyway, I'll go through them at home and figure out which to take on for next week's column."

Lesley, who had known Gabby since they were in preschool together and was completely familiar with how obsessive and stubborn she could be, just smiled. "Well listen, if you get anything really interesting, can I go along when you investigate? The band doesn't have any gigs lined up for a few weeks; I've got to do something to keep life interesting."

"Of course," Gabby said, without pointing out that her so-called band had only ever had a single "gig," and that was at the base player's own birthday party, in his garage last summer. She figured everyone was entitled to their dreams...and delusions.

None of the tips turned out to be anything worth following up on. Two were, as she had guessed, jokes meant to mock her. One was someone who felt her email was their rightful platform for preaching the sinfulness of pagan beliefs in supernatural phenomena. The last two seemed legitimate, but not particularly interesting: a water fountain in Center Hall that would occasionally stop working mid-drink, while other times would respond to the merest touch on its button with a water stream worthy of a firehose ("Sounds like old, bad plumbing more than mysterious forces to me," had been Lesley's helpful comment.) The other was a suggestion that the large, black "W" tiled into the floor in the entrance hall was cursed, and anyone who stepped on it when the moon was full was in for bad luck. That might've been interesting to look into, but without a specific incident and witnesses to interview, she couldn't see how she could use that tip, either. She wrote back to that person, thanking him for his idea and asking him to let her know if he learned of any particular incidents—with witnesses— to support his theory.

By Friday afternoon she was feeling deflated. Only a couple of other tips had come in, and neither of them were useful, either. She had a deadline for her next column looming early the next week, and nothing to write about.

"I guess you're going to have to investigate something you already know about," Lesley said on their way home from school. They were walking, because although Lesley had both her license and a car, she also had a flat tire and no spare.

"I know, but I was hoping for something...recent, fresh, contemporary!"

"I'm sure stuff will come up during the year," she said. "Every year there's buzz about something or other happening around Halloween, right? And then in the spring, with the big theater production...."

Gabby nodded thoughtfully. "Well," she said firmly, "I guess the easiest place to start is with the school nurse story."

"The one the janitors like to scare us by talking about?"

"Mm-hmm. Supposedly she appears when all the lights are off, and the school is empty...so it's going to mean sneaking into the building." She looked at her friend. "Are you in?"

"Sneaking back into the Teen Prison during the island of freedom known as Weekend?" Lesley shook her head. "I must be crazy, but yeah, count me in."

Nurse Myth Debunked

By Roxanne Chance, Investigative Reporter

Two anonymous sources have confirmed a midnight investigation into the story of the Ghost Nurse who roams the halls at night.

Although due to recent turnover, few janitors currently on staff were available for comment, Mr. Jasper Franks agreed to share what he knows about the phenomenon.

"I never saw it myself," Mr. Franks, who has headed our janitorial staff for the past two years, explained last week, "but old Raskins always swore he'd seen her a bunch of times." Horace Raskins, lifetime resident of Roseville and 30-year employee of Roseville Public Schools, spent the last ten years of his career working nights here at WHS. He retired two years ago and was unavailable for comment. "He always said she looked worried," Mr. Franks added, "and seemed in a hurry. He wasn't ever afraid once he'd gotten used to her."

An anonymous account of an attempt to verify this tale was reported early Monday morning. Two people claim to have snuck into the school after midnight this past Saturday, and though they spent all the hours between midnight and sunrise wandering the halls themselves, they encountered nothing resembling the Ghost Nurse.

"We confess to some disappointment," the anonymous email we received stated, "but exposing the truth is more important than cherishing myths which mislead our student body."

We remain open-minded, and willing to hear any further accounts that may occur, but at this time we must conclude that the reports of this haunting are untrue.

"Two anonymous sources?" Ms. Bloom looked over the tops of her glasses at Gabby, eyebrows raised. "These people broke into our school, Gabby. Who are they?"

Gabby lifted her chin and closed her eyes. "A good journalist protects her sources at all costs," she said firmly.

Ms. Bloom shook her head. "You might want to find a good euphemism to use, instead of 'snuck in,' just so no one in administration gets upset about this," she said, handing the manuscript page across her desk. "And perhaps consider the use of the word 'allegedly,' just in case. I also need photos with captions, and a subhead. Deadline is tomorrow."

Gabby was frustrated. Lots of people liked talking to her about her column, but few legitimate leads were coming in—certainly not enough for an investigation every week.

"Why not do some of your columns on, like, background stuff?" Lesley suggested. They were eating lunch together out on the soccer field, enjoying an unusually warm afternoon in late September.

"What do you mean?"

"You know, kind of expand on what you did in your first article." Lesley took a large bite of her sandwich and chewed thoughtfully. "Explain things like lei lines and the history of where the school is built, superstitions, aliens, possible explanations for supernatural things, that kind of stuff. I mean, since you don't have any *actual* occurrences to talk about..."

Gabby lay back on the grass and closed her eyes against the bright sun, enjoying its warmth on her face. "I guess," she said. "I just had such high hopes for this whole project."

But in order to keep up with her weekly deadlines, she had to do something. She followed Lesley's advice and filled her October columns with information about all the different things people come up with to explain the things they don't understand.

The third week of October brought something new.

Gabby was pacing impatiently outside Lesley's 4th period class, waiting for her to be released for lunch. When she appeared, she grabbed her arm and said, "Come on."

"Where are we going? Is there food? I'm hungry."

"Yes, yes, you can eat when we get there," Gabby said, pulling her along and rolling her eyes.

She dragged her all the way across the school, up the stairs, and into the balcony of the auditorium, leading her to the farthest corner seats. Below they could see a few students puttering around doing things on the stage, some racks of costumes and half-painted sets.

"What is this?" Lesley demanded when they were sitting. When Gabby gestured for her to be quiet, she lowered her voice. "What's going on, Gab?"

Without speaking she reached into her bag and pulled out a crumpled wad of paper, smoothed it out, and handed it to her. There was writing on it—the kind where someone had cut out random letters and words from other things and glued them together to spell out a message.

If you want to see some real ghosts, come to the Band Room at midnight on Halloween night. The back door will be unlocked. Tell no one. You won't be disappointed.

"Well okay," Lesley said slowly, handing it back to her. "So...you gonna go?"

"Of course!" Gabby hissed. "But I want a second set of eyes, and that means you." She smiled at her, batting her eyelashes playfully. "That's why we had to be here to talk about this; it says to tell no one, but I had to tell you!"

Lesley reached into her lunch bag and pulled out a bag of potato chips. "Mmm-hmm. Don't you think you could've waited until, like, after school?" She crunched a mouthful of chips loudly, and Gabby hushed her again.

"What do you say? Are you in?"

Lesley took her time answering, eating the chips slowly, with a contemplative look on her face, as if weighing the pros and cons carefully…just to see Gabby squirm a little. "I guess," she grinned, wadded up her bag and threw it at her. "But this time, my cooperation will come at a higher price. I'm talking cookies," she added, poking Gabby in the shoulder for emphasis, "homemade, a whole batch---and no nuts!"

Halloween was on a Wednesday. Gabby had the cookies ready as promised, but Lesley didn't go with her. An early wave of flu was making the rounds, and Lesley came down with it Monday night.

"Are you sure you should do this alone?" Lesley croaked over the phone when she called Gabby with the bad news on Tuesday. "Do you think it's safe?"

"Of course it's safe!" Gabby scoffed. "Don't worry about me. Even if I do actually see a ghost this time, it can't hurt me---it's just a spirit, right?"

"Well, okay," Lesley's voice was fading to a whisper. "But be careful, Gab."

She was careful. She didn't want her parents to know she was sneaking out, so she helped out with trick-or-treaters early in the evening, washed up the dinner dishes, and watched some TV with her little brother, all just as usual. At 10:00 she said good night and went through her usual bedtime routines before closing her bedroom door— and locking it.

At 11:30 she climbed out her bedroom window, scooted along the edge of the roof, and lunged out for the large apple tree growing at the corner of the house. In a matter of moments, she'd clambered down and was flitting from shadow to shadow down the street toward school.

She got there with ten minutes to spare before midnight. She saw no one, heard nothing, and was generally satisfied that everything was normal and deserted. She kept her phone in one hand, ready to video anything that might pop up...or call 911, which ever seemed most appropriate.

The Band Room was actually a small set of buildings behind the auditorium. The back door was, as the note had said, unlocked, and Gabby opened it quietly and sidled inside.

She was in a hallway with no light. She stood still, waiting for her eyes to adjust. Finally, she was able to make out dim shapes at the far end of the hall and began moving toward them. She found her way to a door and up a short flight of steps into the main room. She stood at the outer edge, taking in the rows of chairs and music stands, the instruments in their cases lining the walls and stacked on shelves, straining her eyes to see if anyone else was there, too.

"Are you the reporter?" a raspy whisper came from the other side of a shelf of instruments. Gabby squinted into the darkness, trying to see who had spoken.

"I got a note, telling me to come here," she said softly. "It said I'd see a ghost." She cleared her throat and lifted her chin. "I'm with the WHS Gazette, investigating a tip," she added.

"Are you alone?" the voice asked.

"Yes."

"Follow me." Now she could see a tall, skinny shadow emerge from behind the shelving, and gesture for her to walk across the room toward another doorway.

"Where are we going?" Gabby asked, but the boy---she could tell it was a boy, he was wearing skinny jeans and some kind of black jacket, with a stocking hat covering his head—merely gestured for her to follow again and disappeared through a door into the dark beyond.

He led her down a hall, through another door, and into a stairwell. It seemed like about two stories of downward steps, Gabby thought, and began to feel less sure of herself. "The note said the ghost would be in the Band Room. Where are you taking me?"

The boy looked over his shoulder at her but kept going down. "It's in the basement," he said, a little breathlessly. "We have to get underground to see it."

Gabby checked her phone and was alarmed to see that it was showing no bars of reception. She could still take pictures and video but calling for help was no longer an option. As if sensing her unease, the boy said, "Don't worry. Like the note said, you won't be disappointed."

Gabby squared her shoulders and told herself that this was what investigative reporting was all about: life on the edge, taking a risk for a great story.

At the bottom of the stairs there was another door. The boy held it open for her to walk through. Gabby hesitated for a moment, then stepped past him. The room she entered was dimly lit. It appeared to be an access room to plumbing and heating ducts, maybe furnaces and things like that. Gabby took a few steps forward, ducking under on low pipe, and turned to the boy.

"Okay, we're here," she said, putting her hands on her hips. "Where's this ghost?"

The boy just grinned at her and nodded, as if he was agreeing with her question, which made no sense—but then she felt her elbows grabbed from behind. She dropped her phone in surprise and stumbled backward.

"Oh, don't worry, we're going to have a ghost down here," a new voice, high pitched and shrill sounding, "we're going to make one!"

Pining her arms behind her so tightly it hurt, the new person dragged Gabby across the floor and shoved her down onto a chair. She could feel him tying her wrists behind her back, probably to the chair too.

"Stop!" She cried. "Let me go! People know I'm here---I work for the Gazette! You can't do this—" she tugged at her arms, but the bindings were firm. The first boy was standing a few feet away, grinning that crazy grin and still nodding. "They'll come looking for me—you're going to get into big trouble!"

"Don't worry, precious," the voice behind her murmured. "The only thing left for anyone to find will be a ghost---yours! And isn't that what you're after, anyway? You want to expose all the ghosts of WHS?" He laughed and finally stepped into view.

"Pete McKinney," Gabby said, recognizing him. "Aren't you in enough trouble already?" She was angry now. "After that stunt you pulled at the Homecoming game, you're not supposed to come within 500 feet of school property!" She had been the one to report on the incident for the paper, since Ms. B didn't think her own column was enough to keep her busy. During the first half of the game, Pete and his buddies had snuck into the locker rooms, put dead cockroaches in the cheerleader's clothes, and smeared feces in the football player's things. It wasn't the first time Pete had been in trouble, but it was the final straw for the WHS administration. He'd spent a week in Juvenile Detention, was banned from campus and expelled from the school district. "What's going to happen now that you're adding kidnapping to the list of your offenses---and on school property?!"

Now the first boy had stopped smiling, and was shaking his head in a negative direction, walking toward her slowly. Pete just shrugged and kicked the side of her chair, jolting her and pushing her a foot across the floor. "You can see how worried I am," he drawled. Looking at the other boy, he said, "Get her in position. I'll get the stuff."

Gabby was pushed deeper into the underground room, until she found herself in a large empty space with markings on the floor. She realized it was a pentagram, and there were all kinds of symbols written inside and around it, in red and black.

"What is this?" She demanded, trying to sound angry instead of terrified. "Some kind of Satanic thing?"

Pete laughed quietly and reappeared holding a bag, which he placed on the floor outside the drawing and began unpacking: a variety of knives and small statues and candles came out, and she could feel the hot, shallow breath of the other boy on the back of her neck.

"We're gonna live forever," his whisper rasped against her ears. "Ain't no one gonna be able to touch us!" And she felt the disgusting sensation of his tongue running across the back of her neck.

"Get off me!" She shouted.

"Shut up, Jimmy," Pete snapped. "Come here and help me."

Gabby watched as the bizarre pair placed various things around her, her eyes returning to the glinting edges of the knives which still lay on the ground. She was trying to be smart and calm, trying to think of some way to get herself out of this, but her brain kept shrieking *This wasn't supposed to happen! There was supposed to be a ghost! They're going to kill me!*

"So what are you guys trying to do?" She finally managed to ask, hoping to keep them talking until a better idea occurred to her. "Is this because it's Halloween?"

Pete smirked at her and picked up one of the long blades, running his thumb down the length of it slowly.

"I mean, if I'm about to die, I'd like to know why." *At least I can sound like I have a backbone*, she thought, *even if it's actually turned to jello.*

"You're our ticket," Jimmy piped up from behind her. "You're gonna pay the price so we don't have to."

"I said to shut *up*," Pete snapped at him. "Get over here and light the candles." Pete paced around the edge of the circle while Jimmy clumsily lit the five white candle stubs on the ground, panting shallowly and wiping his hands on his pant legs periodically. When they were lit, Jimmy scuttled backward into the shadows, and Pete lifted his arms, threw his head back, and closed his eyes, tracing shapes in the air with the blade he held while chanting something that sounded like a really screwed up version of Latin.

"Really? Magic words? As if that stuff really means anything!" Gabby heard her voice shaking, but wanted to do something to stop him, distract him.

"Shut up bitch," Jimmy's scratchy voice came from across the room, and then she heard a scuffling sound, and a thud. She would've tried to see what had happened, if he'd tripped or something, but her full attention was on Pete now, who'd stopped chanting and was stepping into the circle, only a couple of feet away from her, blade pointing straight at her throat.

"The blood price is demanded! Mortality for immortality! O Dark Powers we offer our sacrifice!" Pete kind of moaned the words in his squeaky voice, and even as scared as she was, Gabby felt the urge to roll her eyes. *Why do I have to be killed by two morons?!* she thought.

Suddenly the air around her moved. The blade, mere inches from her neck, dropped onto the ground, clattering loudly. All but one of the candles blew out. She could only see the shadowy outline of Pete standing in front of her. "What the—" she heard him say, then a soft, wet sound, like someone biting into a watermelon. The room seemed to hold its breath. Then, almost simultaneously, she heard the unmistakable sound of Pete's body hitting the ground, and felt her wrists being freed from the chair.

"Who's there?" She said, rubbing her wrists and standing up slowly. "Hello?" She didn't understand why, but somehow this felt more terrifying than knowing she was about to be some loser's blood sacrifice.

"You're Roxanne Chance, the girl who writes for the school newspaper." It was a deep voice, a man's voice, and then out of the shadows emerged the person who belonged to it.

"Mr. A? Is that you?" Gabby felt weak with relief, and almost sat down again. Mr. A---short for Annakim—was a math teacher, new to the school that year. Everyone knew about him, even if they didn't have him, because he was considered hot by most of the female population. "What are you doing here?"

Mr. A laughed gently. "I was working late and saw these two sneaking around the parking lot when I went to my car." He had a slight accent, exotic and unidentifiable. His voice was comforting. He held out his hand to steady her, pulling her away from the circle and the chair. "It's a lucky thing I decided to stick around and see what they were up to."

"Am I ever glad you did!" Gabby smiled and felt a surge of energy—no doubt the adrenaline was hitting now that the danger was past.

Then she looked down at Pete.

He lay there, a small pool of blood growing beneath his head, his body twisted in an awkward pose, his eyes staring glassily.

She looked to where she thought Jimmy should have been. There was a lump that might be him, lying on the floor, which also looked suspiciously wet around his head.

Smile gone, she pulled her hand away from Mr. and took a step backward.

"Did you kill them?" her voice sounded very small and frightened in her own ears.

Mr. A looked regretfully at the two shadowed bodies and nodded sadly. "Yes," he said quietly, "I'm afraid so."

Gabby felt greater horror now than she had all night. What was he going to do to *her* now? She was a witness! He'd have to kill her too. Her eyes darted past him, to where she thought the door was, though she was slightly disoriented and not sure she could actually find it.

Mr. A put his hands in his pockets and dropped his chin a little, looking at her from under his dark eyelashes. "I'm not going to hurt you, Roxanne. Do you go by Roxy?"

She shook her head. "Gabby, it's really Gabby." She felt mesmerized by his look, couldn't look away, couldn't not answer.

"Gabby, then." He smiled at her warmly. "You are safe. I'm going to take you out of here, and you'll be all right." He took a few steps in the direction of the door. "Why don't you follow me?"

For the second time that night, Gabby found herself following a stranger through dark rooms, up dark stairs, and into the Band Room. She was shaking so badly by the time they reached the rehearsal hall, she wasn't sure she'd be able to keep walking.

As if he knew this, Mr. A turned around and said kindly, "Why don't you sit down for a minute."

Gabby sat in the nearest chair. She shook her head and tried to move her brain toward something like coherent thought. She didn't feel safe yet, but she was beginning to hope that Mr. A wasn't out to kill her, too.

"What happened down there?" She blurted out at last, the only words she could form, though it seemed to her a thousand questions were crowding into her brain at once.

Mr. A crossed the room to the upright piano that was there and leaned on it gracefully. He smiled at her.

"I will tell you," he said, and Gabby felt herself relaxing, letting the chair back support her. Her breathing slowed. She didn't know what was happening, but she felt that there was no danger, *although safe isn't quite the word for this situation either*, she thought. "I will tell you because you have a fire inside that drives you to seek answers, and those fires are never lit for no reason." Gabby blinked a few times, trying to untangle what he'd just said.

"Thank you, I think," she ventured, and he laughed.

He smiled, and his teeth showed, like pearls in moonlight. "Those boys were trying to harness dark forces in order, I believe, to transform themselves into vampires. They were going to use your blood in their misguided attempt."

"How do you know?"

"I recognize the symbols, their props. They're common enough among fans of the dark arts, and those who fall for the pablum that passes for how-to websites and instruction guides." Gabby opened her mouth to ask another question, *Why do you know this?* but he continued talking. "It would not have worked. You would have died. They probably would have made themselves ill. I think it altogether likely that Peter would have turned on Jimmy, and killed him as well, in the end." He shook his head. The small movement seemed filled with a bottomless grief that Gabby didn't understand. "Their paths were destined for disaster, and now are ended."

"But, sir, *you* ended them. Don't we need to call the police or something? I mean, you were saving me, I doubt you'll get in trouble or anything. I'll be your witness." Gabby leaned forward, forearms on her thighs, and tried to see his face clearly. The whole room was hazy, and she couldn't focus her eyes.

"No, we will not call the police." He smiled again, and Gabby felt the waves of his sadness wash over her. "Let me explain," he held his hands out, palms up, and she felt as if he had pushed her back into her chair, but gently. She sighed as her shoulders drooped back onto the chair. The noisy, confused part of her brain shouting at her that something was wrong was muzzled and distant.

"In case you have ever doubted it," Mr. A began, "there is evil. There has always been evil. It reaches every corner of creation, it infects every part, it knows no boundaries. Where there is light, there are shadows," here he held up a single finger, "but never forget that the light is there, too.

"Some of us have been created, since the Great Beginning, to fight the evil, to protect its would-be victims, to guard against its spread where ever possible." Here he bowed his head and Gabby could hear a soft exhale, again filled with sorrow. "The battle is eternal. But we who are tasked with it are not defenseless. We are given arms, of a sort, and use them where we must." Now he wrapped his arms around himself, as if for comfort. "But with power comes responsibility, and always there is a price to pay."

Gabby stirred. "Sir, I don't understand. Are you talking about Pete and Jimmy? Do you think they were evil? Are you saying it's your job to…kill…people like them?"

Mr. A shook his head. "No, Gabby. They were weak, cowards at heart. And evil is always drawn to weakness like theirs. It uses them to do its work in the world. They are merely the victims, the price *I* must pay in order to do *my* work in this world." Now he looked at her, his eyes silver, glowing, and she felt frozen. "I am a Watcher from the beginning of Time. It is my destiny to protect and defend. In order to do so in *this* world, I have great power, but I must sustain myself at the cost of other life."

He extended one arm and Gabby could see a smear of blood on the inside of his sleeve. Then he lifted his arm to his mouth, and mimed wiping something away, then showed her his sleeve again.

Gabby gasped. "You…did you…are *you* a vampire?!" She felt an hysterical urge to laugh because it was all too ridiculous. She had come tonight hunting a ghost, ready to report it or debunk it. But a *teacher* claiming to be…what? An avenging angel? A vampire?!

"It is our curse." There was that poignant anguish again, welling up within his words. "The tragic irony that we must live at the expense of life in order to fulfill our mission. Guardians and Warriors of Light, we are doomed to contribute to the shadows, though we may try to do so in the least of ways."

Gabby was transfixed. She felt frozen in place, and guessed that this was something he was doing, keeping her there, making her stay. There was still part of her brain that wanted to make sense of this, to question, to find out more. But that part of her brain seemed unattached to her mouth, and though she could think her questions, she could not speak them.

"There are Watchers, Guardians," Mr. A went on, stepping away from the piano and moving toward her slowly, "and there are Seekers. Those who are driven to know, to understand. And there are others as well. Some with other powers, other gifts and abilities. In your world," he was half way across the space that had separated them, and Gabby wondered if she had the power to get up and run, but didn't even try because he was still talking, and she wanted to hear what he had to say, "Seekers have been scientists, storytellers, philosophers. The others are often found among the ranks of artists and outcasts. You are," he was standing only inches in front of her, still holding her gaze with his light-filled eyes, "I believe, one of the Seekers. Which is why I have told you everything."

She felt the moment open to her, and was able to gasp out, "I don't just try to understand, though. I want to tell what I find. I'm an investigative reporter," she still felt a swelling of pride when she heard herself say the words, even knowing that she had no idea if she would ever leave this room. "It's my job to tell."

"I know," Mr. A smiled so tenderly down at her that she almost wanted to cry. She felt that, somehow, he loved her. "That is why I must bury what you know deep, where you won't find it for a long time, because for now you must *not* tell. And I would not subject you to the torture of knowing something that you must not tell."

She opened her mouth to speak but realized that there were no words---all her words had been taken from her---and all she knew was the whirling galaxy of lights within his eyes.

"Gabby, this is good," Ms. B frowned across her desk at her only investigative journalist. "But you seem to be going in a different direction than where you began this column. Almost...philosophy?" She lifted an eyebrow. "Do you think your readers will embrace this?"

Gabby shrugged. She knew it was esoteric, because when she'd run it by Lesley, her response had been, "Too many big words. And ideas. Why not just write about ghosts, like you used to?"

But something inside her made her stick to her guns and write this instead.

"Well," Ms. B handed her the manuscript, now peppered with editing marks and comments in the margins, "fix the stuff I circled, and there are a couple places where you need clarification, but otherwise go ahead and use it." She grinned. "Anyone who leads with Shakespeare gets to publish, as far as I'm concerned."

"Thanks Ms. B," Gabby took back her papers, glancing down at the first few paragraphs.

The Bottom Line:
WHS Mysterious Phenomena
Reexamined

By Roxanne Chance, Investigative Reporter

Shakespeare intermingled ghosts and real people, history and mythology, because he knew a truth that we live every day here at WHS:

> *There are more things in*
> *heaven and earth, Horatio,*
> *Than are dreamt of in*
> *your philosophy.*
> *-Hamlet: I, v*

Mysteries surround us every day. Sometimes they are simple and common.

But some mysteries are grander, and deeper, and we have our share of them here.

She flipped to the second page, scanning the edits and comments, and read just the end, smiling a little.

This column has been an attempt to explore some of these mysteries. In spite of numerous tips, uncountable conversations with many people in our school community, and even a few investigative forays into ghost hunting, answers have remained out of reach.

And that leaves this reporter wondering if maybe that isn't the point?

Perhaps we need some mysteries to keep life interesting, to remind us that we can't know everything, and there is more to this world than meets the eye?

The Bard knew. Maybe we should take a page from his book.

She walked across the classroom to the computer she'd been working on, and sat down to do her editing, when she heard Ms. Bloom say, "If any of you are looking for something to add to your portfolio before the end of this marking period, we need reporters to interview the Mathletes team, as well as their coach, Mr. Annakim. They just won the State tournament and will be going to Nationals next month."

Gabby pulled up her document file and began to make the changes marked on her first draft. As she worked, she thought about what to do for her next project. It wasn't her usual thing, of course, but something about the idea appealed to her. Maybe if she took the angle of their team's success under new leadership, where Mr. A had come from and what he'd done before Washington High, she could make the Mathletes story into something worth spending her time on.

5

THE SPARE ROOM

All the doors up there were supposed to be locked. And they all were. Except the spare room.

Once a month it was Prudence's turn to watch through the night, walking the halls below stairs and up in the attics, making sure no one was sneaking about, getting into the pantry, coming in after hours. They each took it in turn. It was one of the duties that came with the job, common enough for kitchen and house staff in the larger homes.

Mostly it was fine. Boring, and at times difficult to stay awake, but otherwise harmless. Except once a night the upper attics had to be checked. A few of these small rooms tucked away in the upper-most reaches of the house were used for storage: furniture, crates packed with straw to cushion forgotten contents, gathering dust. Most were empty, the rooms unneeded for household staff, numbers being smaller nowadays due to the war. With so many young men off fighting the Germans in His Majesty's army, and women needed as nurses or in the factories, there just weren't enough people to staff the grand manor houses like they used to.

Used or not, all the attic rooms were meant to be closed and locked at all times.

But at the far end of the hall, one door was always open.

Just an inch or two.

The gap was small. But she'd heard things.

Breathing. Ragged panting, like someone in pain.

When she peered at that small, black gap, a pair of shining eyes stared back at her. They seemed mad, evil, malicious, and she'd scurried away as quickly as she could.

Another time she'd quickly pulled the door closed, without looking inside. As she walked away, she heard a low, oily chuckle, followed by the creek of hinges.

She did not look back but ran all the way downstairs.

"You're looking ragged this morning," Mrs. Hankins said as she filled Prudence's teacup.

Ellie Smythe, Prudence's roommate, walked into the dining hall just in time to hear the comment.

"And no wonder," she exclaimed. "She had the night watch last night. Up all hours roaming the empty halls," she leaned sideways and poked Pru in the ribs. "Did you see anything in the Spare Room this time?"

"Tch!" Mrs. Hankins rapped her knuckles against the table and gave Ellie a hard look. "I'll not have such talk in this house." She reached for a platter of eggs and passed it down the table as other servants joined them for the morning meal. "That's the kind of nonsense that causes trouble and has no truth to it." She crossed her arms and added, "This is a Christian house, and there'll be no wicked rumors started below stairs while I have anything to say about it!" She turned on her heel and bustled out of the room.

Groggy morning greetings were exchanged as the staff tucked into their breakfasts. Prudence had the morning off, as was customary after being on night watch, so she lingered over an extra cup of tea as the others hurried off to their various tasks, answering to bells and hurrying so as to avoid the ire of Mrs. Hankins, should they be late. At last, it was just herself and old Joseph, the head groundskeeper, sitting in amicable silence.

Joseph had been born on a nearby farm, come to work as a boy in the stables, and though his job had changed over the years, he never left the estate. He was old now—some claimed he was almost 90, though no one knew for sure—and allowed to go at a slower pace. Even so, he still made sure to check on the work of the lads who worked under his supervision, and the grounds were kept very well.

"Hankins doesn't like to hear of it," he croaked suddenly from the far end of the table, startling Prudence, "but there's some as seen things in that Spare Room."

Prudence felt suddenly wide awake. "Have you, Mr. Joseph?"

He took a long sip of tea before answering. "Haven't been up there since the last Earl died," he said at last, "but before then I took my turn at night's watch, same as everyone. We all knew there was sommat up there. Some saw more'n others."

"What is it?" Prudence clasped her hands and leaned forward. "Every time I'm up there I can feel it…and sometimes I have heard.… sounds…" She'd tried to talk to some of the others about it, but they'd all dismissed her as being a foolish child and warned her not to let Hankins hear her talk.

"It's usually the children," Joseph said, leaning back in his chair and producing a pipe from his pocket. Mrs. Hankins had strict rules about smoking in the house, but Prudence suspected that old Joseph was as exempt from that as he was from most other rules. He struck a match and pulled on the pipe until small puffs of smoke plumed out. "In the old days we had many more young 'uns coming into service, age 7, 8, 9."

"I'm eleven," Prudence said quietly. Her mother couldn't work, and with both her brothers and father gone to war, she was the only one able to provide an income for her mother and younger brother and sister, until the relief checks started to come. She'd been sorry to leave school, but there were no other options. She knew was lucky to have the job at all.

"Aye, I thought as much." Joseph puffed away. "But those who started young and stayed on, we still felt things, saw things."

"Like what?"

"Oh, I 'spect you know well enough," he squinted at her through a haze of fragrant smoke. "But I know how it is: you want to hear that someone else has seen it, too." He nodded and chuckled. "They used to make us older'n swear not to tell the young ones...until they came askin'. Then we could tell 'em everything."

Prudence merely blinked at him, almost holding her breath, hoping he would say more.

"My first night up there, I were only six. I saw the door open, and tryin' to be a good lad, I went to close it. Soon as I got near, I heard a breathing so heavy and wet, it sounded like someone might be dying. Instead of closing it, I pushed the door wide, and saw nothing, but I felt it, all around."

"Like the air was thick, you mean?" Prudence had almost felt frozen in place one night, unable to push away from the dreaded room.

"Aye," Joseph nodded. "And my feet felt stuck. Then I heard a wicked laugh from somewhere behind me—behind the door, in the darkest corner, as I thought at the time. I screamed, because I was young, and I fell over." He tamped some new tobacco into his pipe's bowl, lit it, and puffed a few times before continuing. "'Twas Maisy who found me lying there, stone cold unconscious, next morning. I didn't wake for two days, and they feared I was a goner." He cackled and winked at Pru. "Not me! I came back and got mad, for I was ashamed, even as a small boy, at fainting like a woman! I asked to be on the very next night watch."

There was a sound of feet in the hall and voices of passing servants, louder than usual and sounding perturbed, rushed. It reminded Prudence that she would be expected upstairs at 1:00. She glanced at the clock. She still had 5 hours. Although she yearned for sleep, she wanted to hear more.

"Did you ever *see* anything?" The recollection of shining eyes peering at her across the inky blackness of the room haunted her dreams.

"Aye," Joseph nodded. "Me 'n others. I mostly just heard things--- the breathing, the laughter. But once I saw a shadow move across that open door. Brave as I tried to be, when I thought it was coming out toward me, I ran away." He winked again and went on. "Trevor from the North Country saw more 'n the rest of us. Eyes, he said, evil eyes peering at him from within the room. And one time he swore he saw a phantom bed appear in a shaft of moonlight, when the moon was full and shining in the window as he passed by. Worst of all," he leaned toward Prudence and dropped his voice to a hoarse whisper, "there was sommat in the bed, moving, thrashing about, making great animal convulsions, while the evil laughter carried on and on."

Prudence realized she was trembling and wrapped her arms around herself. "Was anyone ever hurt by the…whatever it is up there?"

Joseph appeared to give a great deal of thought to her question, taking the time to refill his pipe a third time, before answering. At last he said, "No, not in the way you mean. Many of us had a good scare, but nothin' worse than nightmares afflicted us."

Pru had the sense that he was holding something back. "But what, then? Who was hurt?"

"Well," Joseph took a long, deep draw on his pipe and blew the smoke out in rings that floated into the air above his head, "it's the stories we heard about the room I'm thinking of.

"In the days before I came, three Earls ago and longer, when Queen Victoria sat on the throne, all of those attics were filled with servants, sometimes two to a room. In those days the estate was busy as a beehive.

"*That* room, though, was kept empty, a place for visitors who turned up occasionally. Sometimes it was someone applying for work but yet to be hired and assigned a place. Sometimes a family member of one of the staff would stop over and were accorded a single night's lodgings as a courtesy of the Estate.

"It was a golden time, but like all such times it came to an end. The next Earl was born with a stain on his face, red and mottled and horrible. His mother was of a weak constitution, and seeing her deformed child drove her mad. Had to be locked up half the time, she did, and the old Earl died of grief over it---although in truth, he married very late, and it might just have been his time," Joseph seemed almost to be speaking to himself now. "In any event, for a time the Estate was in the hands of his mad widow. She turned out all but the most essential staff, shuttered the windows, locked the rooms, refused visitors, shunned the world. Her deformed son, so the story goes, she kept in the attics—*in the spare room.*" He looked Prudence in the eye as he went on. "It was whispered that she visited him nightly, and those servants who remained would hear horrible sounds from the spare room, though none had the courage to go and see what she did up there.

"Things went on like that for ten years or so, until one morning a grounds man—the only one left, my old master William, who taught me everything he knew before he left this world—found the poor mad woman hanging from a tree in the oak grove. He cut her down, carried her inside to wait for the doctor to come and pronounce death. T'was then that he, the housekeeper, and the head butler realized they would need to check the spare room and see what there was to see at last."

Prudence was gripping her own elbows, hugging herself tightly. "What did they find, Mr. Joseph?"

"It was a pitiable, sickly thing, miss," Joseph said, shaking his head sadly. "Such life as it had been given was marred by deformity and isolation. Poor thing was lying in a bed there, the bolster over its face." His pipe had gone out again, but rather than refill it, Joseph set it on the table and dropped his hands into his lap. "The three of them vowed never to reveal what they found, so as not to smear the family name. It was let out that the boy had always been sickly and died, and his death broke the heart of his poor mother, who died right after. Murder and suicide are not stains any family wants attached to them, miss."

Prudence had gasped when Joseph described the scene in the spare room, and now she nodded her head vigorously. "Of course not, sir. Of course not."

Joseph gave a small stretch and pushed his chair away from the table. "The doctor confirmed the situation, the family were notified, and soon enough a cousin was found who was next in line...under him the house was restored and eventually I came along. And even more eventually, you came along."

"But Mr. Joseph, why do we see these things up there?" It was a tragic story, but Pru couldn't figure out why such tortured souls would return to reenact their own misery.

"Who knows, miss? Guilt? Madness? Grief? Who can tell what laws govern spirits in the next world? Now," he reached for his pipe and placed it back in his pocket, "Hankins will not hear tell of this, and what with our world today, few are the folk who notice anything anymore. It's your youth, I'd wager, that makes you more sensitive, and I thought you deserved to know about it. But I'd advise you not to tell others, nor mention your experiences again if you wish to keep your post." He turned and began to walk away from the table, pausing to say over his shoulder, "I've got to be getting along now, but if you should see something again, come find me and tell me about it, I'll be around the place." He winked kindly at her. "That way you won't feel so frightened or alone with it preying on your mind." With those words he left her alone at the table.

Prudence felt all at once overcome with fatigue. She found her way to her room and fell onto her bed, asleep almost before her head touched the pillow, without bothering to undress.

It was several hours later, long past when she had been due for work, that Ellie wakened her.

"Pru! Prudence! Wake up, you sleepy thing! What are you thinking, sleeping without setting your alarm and missing your duty?!"

Wide awake now, Prudence jumped up. "Oh no! Oh Ellie, am I in trouble? Is Hankins looking for me?"

Ellie wagged a finger in her young roommate's face. "No, but you've benefited from someone else's misfortune. The entire household was thrown out of order today."

"Why?"

"Because Old Joseph, that head groundskeeper—you know who I mean? —they found him dead today! He wasn't in any of his usual haunts. One of the underkeepers needed something from him, and went looking---anyway, they found him in his room, lying on is cot, just as if he were asleep, except he was dead. The doctor said he must've passed sometime in the night." Ellie crossed herself without thinking. "We've all been put onto different tasks all day, and the Earl has been deeply affected, as old Joseph has been on the estate for 80 years, so no one's noticed that you were missing."

"But he couldn't have died last night. I was talking to him just this morning!"

"Nonsense," Ellie shook her head. "You stayed behind in the kitchen when the rest of us went to work, and then you went to bed---Joseph was cold and dead already when we were all eating together. Brrr," she shivered and rubbed her arms, "gives me the chills just to think about it."

Prudence felt the hairs rise on the back of her arms and neck. For a moment she thought she could smell the faint, sweet smell of pipe tobacco.

6

────────

GHOST HUNTER

"Are you sure? Do you really think that's him?"

"Yeah! I mean I think so..."

"Go ask him!"

"No, you go."

"No, you!"

He heard the whispered conversation coming from somewhere behind him and wondered how much longer it would take. Would it be both of them, or just one? Would she have something specific she wanted autographed, or would a bar napkin do?

The first sip of his third Jack and Coke slid down his throat. This bar tender knew how to do it right: plenty of Jack, with just enough Coke to give it that candy taste, but not so much that the bite of the bourbon was lost.

"Excuse me?" A timid voice behind him.

Jesus, she's going to make me turn around, he thought, and took another long sip.

Both of them had come, but one was standing just behind the other, peering at him over her friend's shoulder. She gasped, "I knew it!" then blushed and looked away.

"Are you," the front one began, "I mean, you are Josiah Maximillian, aren't you?"

He held up his right hand. "Guilty as charged," he smirked. These were just kids, pubescent packages of fan worship. He scanned the restaurant to see where their families must be sitting, waiting for them.

"Oh my God!" The front girl squealed, and displayed all of her braces in a wide, star-struck smile. "Your show is, like, my favorite of all time!"

"Thank you," he said, trying not to roll his eyes. He really wasn't in the mood for this. He'd left the crew at the hotel bar in order to get away and not have to talk to anyone for an hour or so. "I'm glad you like it."

"Is it all real?" The quiet one, still standing behind her friend, asked, voice trembling. "I mean, do you use special effects, or do you really see ghosts and other weird stuff?" Her friend turned on her, glowering. "I mean, no offense or anything," she got pale, and began stuttering. "I-I'm just interested in CG and s-stuff like that…so if you … I mean…" she withered under her friend's glare.

"Mr. Maximillian, your show is the best," her friend turned back to him, cheeks blazing. "I believe in everything you do." She smiled again. "I love the story about how you got started because of a real ghost, and what the ancient Native American shaman told you, and all the cool haunted places you've gone ghost hunting!"

"Are you filming here? Is it because of the Silver Mine Ghost?" The other girl practically whispered her reference to the local legend, recently the subject of renewed interest because of a string of murders in the surrounding area.

"I'm sorry," he shook his head and winked, "I can't give you any spoilers, ladies."

The girls squealed simultaneously, and the first one held out a paper napkin. "Could we, I mean, would you mind giving us your autograph?"

He took the napkin and asked their names.

"Tracey and Jill."

He wrote the usual, "Keep the lights on! –Josiah Max," addressed it to both of them, and handed it back.

They twittered their thanks and backed away from him, eventually turning and heading toward the table where their parents were watching.

Joe turned back to the bar, picked up his glass, found it empty, and signaled the bar tender for another one.

"That'll be your fourth," a gravelly voice on his left said.

Without bothering to look, Joe replied, "So?"

He heard the creak of the bar stool as the other man shifted his weight. "I doubt you'll be able to hunt down any spirits when you're already so full of them yourself." The man chuckled softly at his own joke.

Joe decided not to answer. The bar tender put another drink in front of him, and he focused on the burnt caramel liquid, the ice cubes, the buzz of conversation in the restaurant around him. Shooting didn't start until tomorrow afternoon, so even if he woke up with a hangover, he'd be fine by the time it mattered.

He took a sip.

What mattered, what *really* mattered, was this episode.

He'd suffered through the meetings with the showrunners and executive producers about the falling ratings, the likelihood of cancellation if something didn't change. They'd be looking at the numbers after *this* episode to make their decision, and that's why he was trying something new: a simulation of a live show, which they'd stream simultaneously with the broadcast. They planned to let viewers vote to decide certain aspects of what he did, which meant pre-filming several different scenarios. It was more expensive to shoot the extra scenes, and it was going to take two more days than usual for shooting and then editing in the "ghosts," but the gamble was worth it.

He hoped.

Because without "Ghost Hunting: Take It To The MAX!" he wasn't sure what else there was for him.

The whole gig had come about by accident. A couple of faked videos he and his buddy Ben made on Halloween four years ago…a sudden YouTube sensation…a phone call from a network headhunter…and Joseph MacMillan was transformed into Josiah Maximillian, ghost hunter extraordinaire.

And if it dried up?

Back to…what? He didn't want to return to college now any more than he had when he dropped out a decade ago. But working at his father's hardware store had been misery, and he would rather live in a cardboard box than go back to that.

"You're not a bad actor," the man on the next bar stool interrupted his thoughts. "I've seen one or two of your shows. They're garbage, of course, but you yourself---you have something, my lad."

Joe could tell by the over-precision of his words that he wasn't American, but he couldn't guess the accent.

"Garbage?" He said, still looking straight ahead, raising the glass to his lips.

"Of course!" That low chuckle rumbled behind the words. "Nonsense. Pure fiction. Fantasy—and mind you, not particularly good fantasy. Do you have writers, or is it all—how do they say it now? —by the seat of your pants?"

He was clearly trying to get a rise out of him, but why? Whatever his game was, Joe didn't feel like playing. It was time to shut this guy down.

"Look," Joe swiveled toward him, looking at him for the first time. "If you've seen the shows, you know we only hunt real ghosts, in historically authentic haunted places." He folded his arms across his chest and leaned back.

"Like here? This town?"

"The old silver mines outside of town, actually, but yeah." He reached for his glass and almost drained it. "Enjoy your little critique, buddy, 'cause it doesn't matter to me. It's the people who watch that matter, and they love this stuff."

A bushy grey eyebrow rose an inch or so up the old man's forehead as he tucked his chin and said, "You mean, they used to, don't you?"

Jesus, who is this guy? Joe shook his head once, then turned away. "What's the matter old man, don't you believe in ghosts?"

"Ah," it was more of a sigh than a word. From the corner of his eye, Joe saw the old man signal the bar tender, and watched as he was brought two shots of something. "That is an interesting question, isn't it?" He slid one of the shot glasses toward Joe. "Why would someone who doesn't believe in ghosties and ghoulies and things that go bump in the night create a whole television program about finding them? And go to the trouble of making up a false history for himself? And fake the supernatural findings of his 'hunting'?"

Joe just shook his head. "No comment." This guy could be wearing a wire or something, trying to do some scandal story for a gossip rag. Best to just ignore him.

"You see Joe," the man continued in a friendly way, as if they knew each other well, "often what people *pretend* to be gives insight into what they wish they *could be.* So perhaps you, in the midst of your chicanery and snake oil sales to the gullible public hungry for deeper meaning in their desperate lives, are actually looking for ghosts. Real ones." He took the shot glass in front of him and tossed it back.

Joe eyed the glass close to him. His Jack and Coke was gone, and at this point the warm, everything's-going-to-be-all-right feeling it had helped create felt like it needed a boost.

"What is that?"

"Jägermeister. Go ahead. Drink it."

He did. It was hard and smooth, and made him think of the darkness between tall trees at night. He shuddered.

"So, what now? Are you going to tell me your ghost story, old man?"

"Joseph my boy, I could tell you stories that would keep you awake every night for the rest of your life." He leaned close and lowered his voice. "But that's not what I'm here for."

The room seemed a little off-kilter, and Joe wondered what proof that Jägermeister was. "What are you here for, then? Just to bother me?" He sniggered, but the old man's face remained serious.

"I'm going hunting. I thought you might like to come along."

Joe peered up at a TV screen showing a muted news broadcast. "It's after 11:00---who goes hunting at this hour?" He straightened himself in his chair and leaned onto the bar, trying not to let his dizziness show.

"You of all people should know the answer to that question, Joseph," the man smiled at him, but only with the corners of his eyes. "If you wish to join me, it's time to go."

The long walk through frigid night air chased away any lingering effects of the alcohol. It wasn't a big town, as most old mining towns weren't, and they'd left it long behind them. Now they were trudging through scrubby winter chaparral, heading toward wilder back country, where mountains began their rise from the valley floor. The rocks were hard, and the trees were thick and old. All the abandoned silver mines were higher up, but Joe's companion wasn't leading him in that direction, instead keeping among the trees and deeper forest trails.

"We'll be taping up there tomorrow," Joe said, panting lightly. "Why not just wait and go in with me then?"

"You do all your filming in daylight?"

"Mostly, yeah."

"So filters and other devices create the illusion of dark for your viewers?"

"Well, we can do that when we need to, sure," Joe still wasn't comfortable telling this guy trade secrets.

The old man stopped until Joe was caught up and standing beside him. "We need real darkness for real ghosts." He held Joe's eyes in a steely gaze before continuing on.

Why did I ever agree to this? Joe shook his head and followed. *It must've been that Jagerstuff he gave me. Then again,* he squinted up into a night sky that was pricked with stars and filled his lungs with the bracing, clear air, *at least I'm not tossing and turning on a lumpy hotel mattress. This beats LA any day of the week.*

"Shh!" The other man held his arm out to signal Joe to stop. They were somewhat higher now, on a path with a bit of a precipice falling off to their left, and he was staring down at the ground below them.

Joe squinted into the darkness, and thought he saw something yellow glinting in the bushes. "What is that?"

"Police tape. It means we are getting close. Come."

They continued walking for some minutes, but more slowly, stepping with caution. The path they followed made a sharp turn around a craggy outcropping of rock. When they rounded it, Joe saw a shallow cave in the side of the mountain.

"Here," the old man whispered, gesturing for him to follow as he clambered over the small boulders and through the scrub, up toward the cave.

When they were safely within, Joe said, "This doesn't look like part of a mine."

"Very observant, Joseph," the old man smiled grimly at him. "Nor is it. However, it is just the place we need in order to snare our quarry." He had produced from under the long coat he wore a satchel, which he began to unload. Joe watched in silence as the man pulled out dark glass vials, a bundle of sticks, some stones, and various other things he might almost have picked up from the ground along the way: feathers, a clod of dirt, a bit of fur which, Joe realized as he looked more closely, was actually a dead rodent of some kind. He shuddered and wondered again just what he'd gotten himself into.

"Hey," he suddenly spoke, "How'd you know my real name? I never told you. And what's your name, by the way?"

"Much is there to be seen by those with clear vision," he muttered obscurely, as he was arranging his things in two piles. "You may call me Abraham."

"Abraham," Joe said to himself. "All right, Abraham. What are you doing?"

"Do you follow the news, Joseph?"

"Yeah, sure."

"Then you must have heard about the string of murders in this area over the past year."

"Of course. That's why we decided to shoot the episode—rumors of the Silver Mine Ghost. We figured we could spin the episode as kind of an NCIS thing, ghost hunting and murder-solving, get more viewers that way." He watched Abraham construct a small teepee of twigs and sticks, as if for a miniature campfire. "We wanted to get here and do this fast, before the police catch up with the real murderer."

"Local folk wisdom is often deeper than it is given credit for," Abraham said, striking a match and holding it to the wood. Joe watched the flame gutter, then spring up as the dry twigs and sticks caught. When the flames were steady, Abraham at last looked up, across the fire at Joe, and sat back on his heels. "The police will never find the murderer because it is not a human being. It may occupy human bodies in order to work its evil in the world, but it is not human itself. This is what we have come for tonight, Joseph: we must capture and destroy this thing before it can do further harm."

For a moment, not longer than a second really, Joe believed him. Then something in the small fire popped, and Joe shook his head. "Come on old man. This has been a nice little nature walk, but it's late, I have to shoot tomorrow, and the fantasy is over. Let's climb back down and call it a night. Nice try, you had me there for a second, but you can't kid a kidder, man."

Abraham smiled, a grin that slit across his face and carried no mirth. "I would not recommend a walk through this area at this time of night alone. No, I would not." He shook his head, still grinning. "Why not wait for me to complete my task, and we will leave together, eh?" He cocked his head to the side. "Humor an old man?"

Joe rolled his eyes and sat on the ground. "Fine. What do you want me to do?"

Abraham dropped the grin and nodded with satisfaction. "Good. I will tell you. You will see. Then you may decide what you believe." He handed Joe a feather, two rocks and what looked like a bunch of small bones. "Place these around the fire when I tell you. Otherwise stay quiet and do not get in the way."

From another pocket, Abraham pulled out a small draw-string bag. He reached into it and sprinkled something over the fire. The flames changed color from yellow gold to blue and green, and seemed to leap higher.

Then he began to chant. Heavy words, deep and hard sounding, in no language Joe had ever heard before.

He sprinkled more sand. The flames became purple with hearts of white.

The chanting grew louder, kind of a song from deep in the old man's chest, echoing against the cave walls.

A third sprinkle from the bag and the flames darkened from purple to black, now reaching almost three feet into the air. Joe suddenly realized that not only was the fire smokeless, it was silent.

Now Abraham pointed to the feather in Joe's hand, and he placed it beside the fire. Next, he pointed to the rocks, and Joe put them beside the feather. They had strange, stick-figure carvings on them. *Runes?* Joe thought.

Another verse of the song, words rolling over each other, and without being told, Joe placed the small bones beside the other things.

Abraham suddenly shouted three times, pounding his fists into the earth.

There was silence. Joe watched his companion stand, holding his arms out, hands open, eyes closed, as if feeling the air for something. Suddenly the purple flames dropped into the coals, and a thick black smoke rose from the campfire. Joe realized the temperature in the cave had dropped, and even the blood in his veins felt sluggish and ice-choked. Across from him Abraham remained standing, but now held something in his palm. It was the dead rodent. As Joe watched, it began to move. He realized that Abraham was now chanting under his breath, muttering those strange words in a singsong whisper. The tiny creature began to writhe, and then make noise: a tiny sound, low at first like a squeaky hinge, then rising until it felt like a needle in his head, his ears, his eyes, and Joe wanted to scream, to blot it out.

Without warning, Abraham flung the small thing into the heart of the fire. The sound stopped at once, to Joe's relief. He blinked across at Abraham, but the old man was staring at the smoke, watching it warily. Joe followed his gaze and realized that it was taking shape, becoming something.

Abraham gestured for Joe to stand up and move to the back of the cave, which he did. The smoke looked evil, roiling, and rotten, emitting a smell that made Joe think of death, slime and mold and hungry insects burrowing into fetid piles of refuse and filth. When he was as far away as he could get, Abraham standing between himself and the smoke, he could see there was a form to it: eyes, though they kept moving, and something like wings, or arms, or tentacles—it shifted constantly, but clearly gave the impression of a creature of some kind.

"Ecthros, I summon thee!" Abraham's voice rang out in the cave. "Thou hast crossed the boundaries set in place in ancient times. Thou hast violated the sanctity of the souls of the living. Thou hast taken life that was not thine to take. I come to send thee out of this world for all time!"

The smoke creature seemed to throw its head back and howl, sounding like a hurricane wind. Looming higher, it leaned over Abraham, curling tendrils of smoky arms around his legs. It seemed to speak with a voice that rumbled like an earthquake, its words scoring the air around them, sharp and incomprehensible. It enveloped the old man, as if eating him, and Joe felt a sickening certainty that he was next.

The irony made him wince: killed on a ghost hunt, a *real* one—the ratings potential would be astronomical—but no one would know, and when he didn't show up for taping the next day, the show would be as dead as he was.

Everything went black. Joe was sure this was the end, when something flashed—light on metal, shining, cutting through the dark. The smoke began to pull back, and he could see Abraham standing there, holding a large, heavy-looking medallion. He raised it up to the smoke, and it recoiled.

"Utukku! Hades! Kokytos!" Abraham chanted strange words, holding the medallion up to the writhing smoke. "Osiris! Eshu! Mictlantecuhtli! Guede!" He took a step toward it, seeming to push it backward and down with the force of his words. "Aipaloovik! Asto-Vidatu! Namtar! Azrael!" Joe felt the air within the cave shudder as the smoke began to lose shape, folding in upon itself. "Magwayen! Fan Wujiu! Yeomra! Erio! Xargi! Thanatos!" Now Abraham was standing directly over the spot where he'd built the small fire, the smoke thinning before him, dwindling. "Odin! Arawn! Aita! Chitragupta! Whiro!" Falling to his knees, Abraham smashed the medallion down onto the coals, smothering them and quenching the smoke entirely.

Silence.

Joe could see the old man's back moving as he drew in deep draughts of air, like a winded runner at the end of his race. He waited for what felt like a long time before, finally, he ventured a few steps forward. When Abraham didn't move, Joe crossed the short distance to him and put his hand on his shoulder.

"Abe? Abraham?" He shook his shoulder gently. "Are you alright?"

Abraham leaned back, pulling the sooty medallion off the pile of burnt sticks and sitting back on the ground. "We're not quite done," he said, still sounding a little breathless.

Five minutes later Joe was standing at the back of the cave, holding a smoldering bunch of dried herbs, waving it up and down and turning in a slow circle.

"Cleansing your work space is an important part of any job," Abraham said to him, as he gathered things from the ground and put them into his satchel. "That's one of the first lessons you must learn."

"First?" Joe paused in his movement and turned back around to face Abraham.

"Keep going, keep going," Abraham waved his arm at him. "All things in good time."

When Joe had gone in a complete circle and Abraham had all his things tucked away, they clambered down from the cave to the rocky path, heading back the way they came. They walked in silence all the way back to town, stopping at the first street light.

"Here I leave you," Abraham said, extending his hand. "Thank you for your help."

Joe took his hand and shook it without thinking. "What the hell was all that?" he stuttered out, as the older man let go of his hand. "What were those things you were saying? What was that smoke?" Joe felt questions bubbling up through the silence and shock of the past several hours, but closed his mouth when Abraham held up his other hand.

"It is nearly sunrise. Now is not the time for questions." He smiled with the corners of his eyes again. "Go and do your work. See what happens. Perhaps another night we shall meet again, and then you will ask your questions. In the meantime," he stepped backward so that he stood outside the pool of light from the streetlamp, his face shadowed now, only his eyes still visible, "I have business elsewhere."

Joe saw him turn and go, watched as he seemed to evaporate into the shadows even as the first blushing light of dawn crept over the rooftops of the town.

He realized that he was freezing. Shoving his hands in his pockets, he turned to walk back to his hotel.

Inside his pocket, his left palm curved around something. He pulled it out to see what it was.

Catching the morning light, a circular metal disc rested in his hand. It was heavy, marked with intersecting lines that formed a pattern in the center, around which there were words—names? Was it Latin?

It left sooty streaks on his fingers. He held it up, turned it over, traced the patterns etched in iron.

He shivered.

Placing it back in his pocket and looking one last time over his shoulder, the held onto the medallion, walking the last silent steps to his room.

7

SÉANCE

"They're here! They're here!"

Looking out of her bedroom window, Amelia watched the cars pull up to the front of her house, delivering her five best friends carrying sleeping bags, pillows, and over-night bags. Her little brother Sam was dancing on his tiptoes at the threshold to her room.

"I know, Sam," she said into the window, seeing her friends greet each other as they traipsed to the front door, waiving to their parents as the cars pulled away. One of them looked up toward her bedroom window, saw her silhouetted there and waived, squealing her name. Amelia grinned and waived back.

"This is a *girls'* sleepover—no boys allowed," she said as she hurried past her little brother on her way down to greet them. "Especially seven-year-old brothers!"

"I know..." he sniffed sadly, but Amelia knew their parents had promised him that he could stay up and watch any movie he wanted, so she wasn't going to feel too sorry for him.

Dharma and Jess were standing arm in arm in front of the door, with Tabia, Meg and Bryony trotting up behind them, laughing because Meg had nearly tripped over a pine cone, and everything is funny when you're with your best friends on the first Friday night of summer.

Giggles and conversation spilled inside with them, through the door and up the stairs. Tossing aside bags and pillows, they were hugging and laughing and talking all at once. Today was Amelia's 11th birthday, but they were also there to celebrate the end of their 5th grade year. Tabia pulled something out of her backpack and hid it behind her back.

"Guess what I've got!" she exclaimed.

"Tabby," Amelia protested. "We said no presents! Tonight is just for being together and having fun!" The other girls got quiet. They'd followed the no presents rule. What if Tabia had gone and brought something for Amelia, after all?

"No, no, silly," Tabia laughed. "Look!" She held out a large wooden box.

"What is it?" Bryony asked, stepping closer, reaching out to touch it.

Tabia sat on the floor and set the box down in front of her. "Open it," she said to Amelia.

It was about twelve inches square, and the wood was dark with age, carved in a leafy relief worn smooth around the edges. "It's pretty," Amelia said, lifting the lid. Inside. it was lined in purple velvet. One of the girls said, "Oooh!" and Meg ran her finger tips over the soft fabric. Nestled in the velvet was a rectangular piece of wood, and beside it a rounded triangle with a glass piece in its center. Amelia looked around at the other girls, and then at Tabia. "What is it?"

"None of you guys have seen something like this before?" They all shook their heads. "Look," Tabia lifted the wood out and unfolded it, showing that it was hinged, and inside covered with symbols, letters, and numbers. "It's a Ouija board!"

Dharma gasped and Jess made a hissing sound.

"What's Ouija?" Bryony asked.

"Just silly superstition," Jess said, reaching for the triangle piece. "See here? You put this on the board," she demonstrated as she spoke, "and everyone is supposed to touch it at the same time."

"Oh yeah! I've heard of these things," Amelia exclaimed. "Then you ask it questions, and the spirits push it around while everyone is touching it, answering the questions by spelling things out!"

Jess rolled her eyes. "It's ridiculous. Totally fake."

Amelia grinned at Tabia. "I love things like this! Thanks for bringing it."

Tabia nodded. "I knew you'd like it. We promised no presents, but since it *is* your birthday, I thought we could do something fun that you'd like, something unusual."

"Something we'll always remember," Bryony said quietly, picking up the pointer piece and turning it over in her hands, looking at it closely.

"How do we do it? Are there rules?" Dharma asked.

"How can there be rules to something that's make-believe?" Jess folded her arms and rolled her eyes again.

"Oh, come on, Jess," Amelia playfully shoved her shoulder.

"You don't have to be the science geek 24 hours a day," Bryony looked over her glasses at Jess, like a grumpy librarian. Dharma giggled. "Just think of it as a game—games don't have to be true, they're just fun!"

Tabia answered Dharma's earlier question. "Sure, there are rules. My grandmother taught me. It has to be dark. We will need a candle. We have to sit in a circle. And there's an ancient incantation to say before we ask questions and lay hands on the *planchette*." She wiggled her fingers dramatically.

Dharma shivered. "Sounds kinda scary."

"Well first," Amelia said, standing up and pulling Dharma up with her. "Mom's got pizza in the oven. And then cake and ice cream!"

******

By the time they were done eating, night had fallen. Fireflies hovered in the darkness under the trees, and a sliver of moon was visible overhead.

"Is it dark enough for your Ouija game now?" Meg asked, dipping her fingers in a puddle of melted ice cream on her plate and licking them.

"I think so," Tabia squinted out the window, "I can see the moon and a couple of stars, even though there's still a little light out there."

"The purple hour," Dharma put in, "that's what my auntie calls this time of night." Her aunt had recently come from India to live with them, and Dharma worshipped her.

"Where should we do it?" Amelia asked.

Tabia pursed her lips. "I think outside, close to nature. Grandma says the natural world is the best place to reach out to the Spirits."

Jess snorted, and Bryony elbowed her in the ribs. "It's not too humid tonight," she said. "And I saw fireflies earlier---it'd be so magical to be surrounded by fireflies, with the stars above us…"

"I'll get a candle," Amelia pushed her chair away from the table and stood up. "Anything else we need?"

15 minutes later all six girls went out the back door, down the stairs and headed into the gloom of the woods behind the house. Dharma had a baggie with a small slice of pizza that Tabia said to bring. Meg carried a thick, wool blanket for them to sit on. Bryony had a white pillar candle and matches. Tabia led the procession, carrying her box.

"We need to find a place away from the lights of your house," she said as they passed the first trees.

"Look out for poison ivy!"

Meg stumbled. "There's a big tree branch there, you guys."

"Eew, I just stepped on something mushy!"

There was a chorus of disgusted shrieks and laughter.

They crossed a small stream, each taking her turn walking across a narrow plank, and followed the landscape as it descended gently into a kind of gully, then climbed again. Finally, Tabia stopped. She looked around, nodding, as the other girls caught up. "This looks good."

They were well beyond the outskirts of the woods. A thick screen of trees made any of the neighborhood houses invisible, though the sounds of suburbia still dimly reached them: somewhere music played, and they could hear cars driving by, distantly and out of sight.

But close around them crowded the evening murmurs of woodland: frogs peeping, the gentle trickling of the stream they'd crossed to get there, and winking in and out of sight, fireflies.

"It's perfect," Bryony sighed.

They spread the blanket on the ground and sat in a circle. Amelia found a flat stone and put it in the middle, placing the candle on it. Tabia opened the box, took out the board, unfolded it, and put it next to the candle. She set the planchette in the center of the board, then looked around at the other girls.

"My grandma told me there's a way to do this," she began, "that she learned from her grandmother, and was passed to her from *her* grand-mother. She says the tools have changed, but the tradition of spirit talking goes all the way back to Africa, and our ancestors were shamans before slavery took them."

"Does your grandma talk to spirits now?" Meg asked eagerly.

"Only when she needs to," Tabia nodded. "She says it's not to be over-done, but it's all right to reach out from time to time."

"So how do we do this?" Amelia pushed up her sleeves and leaned forward.

"First we light the candle."

Dharma picked up the matches, struck one and held it to the wick. Soon the candle glowed. Shadows danced over their faces.

"Dharma, put the pizza beside the candle."

"What's it for?"

"It's our offering to the spirits."

"I hope they like pepperoni," Jess giggled. Bryony told her to hush.

"Everyone scoot in," Tabia instructed, "We all have to be able to put our fingers on the planchette."

The girls drew closer till their knees were touching.

"Now I have to say an opening prayer— "

"I think it's called an *invocation*," Jess interrupted.

"How would you know?" Bryony demanded. "I thought you didn't believe in this kind of thing!"

"Just because I think it's nonsense doesn't mean I don't know anything about it," Jess lifted her chin defiantly. "Ignorance is no substitute for— "

"Okay, okay," Amelia patted her on the knee and smiled. "We get it, Jess, we do."

Tabia cleared her throat and shot a severe look at Jess. "The spirits can refuse to come if someone is an unbeliever," she said. "If you really want to be scientific about this, Jess, you have to keep an open mind."

Jess sighed.

Tabia nodded, then straightened her back and closed her eyes, holding her hands out to either side. "Everyone hold hands," she commanded. Then, in a sing-song voice, she chanted,

> *"E bah shay A-goon*
>
> *E-bah shay a-way*
>
> *E-ray ala-fee-ya*
>
> *E-ray lear-ray*
>
> *E-ray oh-re ray*
>
> *A-way mo dew-pa-we ah-shay*
>
> *O beloved Spirits,*
>
> *We bring you gifts from life into death.*
>
> *Commune with us and move among us."*

There was a hush among them for a few moments. Then Bryony whispered, "That was beautiful. What was it?"

"An ancient Yoruban song to honor and welcome ancestors," Tabia whispered back. "Grandma taught me. Now," she eyed each girl in the circle, "we've opened the door, and it's time to ask a question. Then we each place a finger on the planchette and see if we receive an answer!"

"What should we ask?"

"Let's make it simple."

"I don't know..."

"What about, 'Is there anyone out there?'" Jess spoke up. The other girls nodded. Tabia closed her eyes, breathed in deeply, and repeated the question in a deep voice. Opening her eyes, she placed the forefinger of her right hand on the edge of planchette and nodded at the others to do the same.

It was quiet. With wide eyes, the girls watched the triangle beneath their fingers, each of them aware of the distant noises of daily life. A dog barked somewhere. There was the whispering sound of water nearby and a gentle wind moving the tree branches overhead. Suddenly Meg gasped, "Oh!"

The planchette was moving.

"Keep your fingers in place!" Tabia ordered. "Just let it go where it wants!"

Slowly it moved until the round glass piece in the center was sitting atop a word on the board.

Yes.

"Oh my gosh," Bryony sighed.

"Did one of you push it?" Amelia asked, but her voice shook because she hadn't felt any pressure—none of them had.

Everyone shook their heads. Jess whispered, "I've never felt anything like that."

"Ask another question," Tabia said.

"I will," Dharma leaned forward, as if speaking to the board itself. "Who are you?"

"It's not the board, Dharma," Meg said. "The spirits are around us---"

"Shhh!"

"It's moving again!"

Slowly the planchette slid across the board and settled over a series of letters.

"Z…. E…. D…." It stopped.

"Zed?" Amelia looked around.

"Why are you here?" It was Bryony who asked this time.

The candle guttered for a moment, drawing the girls' attention, until movement at their fingertips drew their eyes back. The planchette was moving across the board to a small drawing of a human head with open mouth.

"It wants to talk to us!"

The girls shivered.

The planchette moved again, this time back to the alphabet letters. It pointed seven times.

"Message?" Jess said the word aloud, and they looked at each other in the candle light with wide eyes.

Meg, who had been very quiet so far, whispered, "What is it?" Everyone knew the question was for Zed.

Everything was still. Each girl kept a finger on the planchette. Their eyes darted from the board to each other and back again as they waited for something to happen. The moments stretched out in silence. Suddenly there was a loud rustling sound in the bushes a few feet away shook. A weird wheezing hough sound followed, and one of the girls yelped.

"It's all right!" Amelia said quickly. "That's just a deer. They're all over the woods back here. I've heard them make that sound before."

"A deer?"

"Are you sure?"

"I've never heard deer make sounds like that!"

"It's true," Jess said, calmly. "That's the sound deer make if they feel threatened and want to scare something away." She grinned halfway and said, "Last year my cat came too near a doe and its fawn, and the doe got really angry. She started stomping and huffing like that, and my cat ran away faster than anything I've ever seen."

There was a murmur of acceptance, amusement, relief.

Then Dharma asked, "I wonder what it was afraid of?"

"You guys!" Tabia hissed.

The planchette was moving again.

They all watched as it pointed to a series of symbols and letters.

"The rose," Meg murmured.

"Now it's spelling something— "

"S, O, R, Y..."

"I think that means 'sorry'."

It moved away from the alphabet letters and diagonally across the board, to a series of stick-like figures lined up like primitive symbols.

"Those are runes," Tabia whispered. It stopped over one. "That one's called 'othilia,' and grandma says it means separation." The girls gazed at the board, looking closely at the other runes around it, wonder filling their minds, when the planchette moved again.

"Letters again," someone breathed the words softly.

They watched.

"*Little*. I think it spelled out 'little,' did you see that too?" Amelia asked when it stopped. The other girls nodded, but the planchette was moving again—over to the numbers this time. It came to rest on the number 1.

Another long pause. Jess blew her breath out loudly, and the candle flame guttered.

"Maybe it's done?" Bryony suggested.

But once again they felt movement under their fingers. The wooden piece glided slowly across the board, settling so that it pointed at the beautiful image of a heart wreathed in flowers and vines, right in the center of the board.

They waited for several more minutes, but nothing more happened. Around them the shadows deepened. The fireflies were high up in the trees and they could feel dew beginning to settle around them.

"Let's say goodbye," Tabia said. And this time they all pushed the planchette with their own strength to the bottom of the board, over the word "Farewell" written in a curling script. "Spirit of our ancestor, we thank you for coming to speak with us and share your message. We wish you peace and love," Tabia spoke in a hushed voice, and when she lifted her finger the other girls did too, sitting back on their heels.

"Wow," Dharma said.

"It's gotten so dark!" Meg's voice squeaked slightly, and Bryony giggled nervously.

"Let's pick everything up and get back to the house," Amelia said, blowing out the candle and standing up.

They moved slowly back through the woods, having more trouble picking out the way because nobody had thought to bring a flashlight. Soon they could see the lights of Amelia's house winking through the tree branches. First one, then another, then all of them ran to the edge of the woods, bursting through the trees onto the clear, grassy slope that was the back yard. They hurried up the deck stairs and ran, breathless, inside.

It was past midnight when they finally ran out of things to say about school, teachers, friends, memories, next year and what middle school would bring, summer plans. Clustered on the floor of Amelia's bedroom in their sleeping bags, the girls gradually fell quiet. Two of them were dozing off when Jess said, "I just can't get over how it moved."

"What?" Meg asked, but they all knew what Jess was talking about, and suddenly no one felt sleepy.

"It really didn't feel to me like any *one* of us was pushing it, you know?" Jess went on. "It was as if it had a mind of its own and was just using energy from our fingers to get where it needed to go."

"Doesn't sound very scientific to me," Tabia teased.

"I know," Jess shrugged. "I can't explain it any better than that, though."

"What do you think it meant?" Bryony wondered aloud. "I mean, was Zed's message for one of us?"

"I wondered if he meant he was bringing a message from someone else, another spirit?" Dharma put in.

"There didn't seem to be anything dangerous in it."

"Yeah, no threats or spooky hints about dead bodies or anything."

"But the deer was afraid of something…"

"That could've been anything! A raccoon or 'possum or something. It didn't necessarily have anything to do with Zed."

"Well, it all seemed pretty random to me, honestly," Tabia said matter-of-factly. "I was hoping there'd be something…more understandable." She yawned. "I'll ask grandma about it when I get home," she offered. "Maybe she can make sense of it."

"Maybe some of those symbols mean something besides what we think they mean," Amelia suggested. "Ask her, then tell us what she says."

They all agreed that was a good idea. One by one they fell asleep.

The next morning the girls woke up one at a time, dozing and whispering until the smells of pancakes and bacon rose up the stairs and crept into the room, watering their mouths and making their stomachs growl.

Amelia's mother and father had set the table and were already stacking food on the five plates by the time they emerged. The kitchen filled with happy girl sounds punctuated by the clinking of silverware on dishes. Most of them had slowed down and were leaning back comfortably in their chairs, sighing with contentment, when a car horn sounded from outside.

"Meg, I think that's your mom's car," Amelia's mother said.

A flurry of activity as the girls jumped up from the table and went to roll up sleeping bags and gather belongings. By the time they were done, three more parents were downstairs, chatting with each other as they waited for their daughters.

Hugs, laughter, more hugs, promises to get together soon, and "See you at the swimming pool!" Only Tabia and Bryony were left. Amelia's parents began cleaning up the breakfast dishes, the girls helping to clear the table.

"When will you see your grandma, Tabia?" Bryony asked.

"I think she's coming for dinner this Sunday," Tabia said, gathering dirty silverware and carrying it to the dishwasher.

"You have to text us and let us know what she says the message meant!" Amelia grinned as she gathered napkins.

"What message?" her father asked.

"Tabia brought a Ouija board, and we tried it out in the woods last night," Amelia explained.

"It was cool—nothing scary or anything, but we got a *message*," Bryony added, with a shivery emphasis that made Tabia grin.

"We're not sure what it meant, though," she shook her head and shrugged. "My grandma knows about these things, so I'm going to ask her. It's her board."

"What was the message?" Amelia's mother asked, rinsing dishes and placing them in the dishwasher.

"Well," Amelia said as she handed her mother dirty plates, "First we found out that the spirit talking to us was named Zed."

"And that he had a message for us," Bryony said.

"But we're not sure if it was from him or another spirit—that's one of the things I have to ask about."

"And…" Amelia's father prompted.

"Oh, the message was a mix of words and symbols. First it pointed to a picture of a rose, and then spelled the word 'sorry,'" Amelia began.

"Then it pointed to a rune that means 'separation,' we think, followed by the word 'little,'" Bryony continued.

"And at the end," Tabia jumped in, "the number 1 and the heart symbol, which I think means love but I could be wrong about that."

A car pulled up outside, followed by another, and Tabia and Bryony hurried to get their things.

The house was quiet with all the girls gone, and Amelia flopped happily down on the sofa in the family room.

"That was a great party," she sighed with satisfaction as her parents walked into the room. "Thanks for letting me have them all over, Mom and Dad." Her parents smiled briefly, but Amelia noticed that they seemed uncomfortable, and her mother especially looked like she hadn't slept much. "Did we keep you up?" she asked.

They sat on either side of her, and her mother took her hand and looked away, shaking her head. Her father spoke.

"No, sweetheart." He put an arm around her shoulders. "We got some bad news last night and didn't want to tell you while the girls were here."

Amelia sat up, rigid, scared of what she was about to hear. "What? What is it?! Where's Sam?"

Her mother took a deep breath that sounded more like a sob and squeezed her hand.

"Sam's fine, but he's sleeping in, he didn't get much sleep last night. He was awake when we got the call, and we had to tell him," her father explained. "Grammy died yesterday, sweetie," her father kept speaking. "It was sudden, a heart attack. She didn't suffer."

Grammy was her mother's mother. Now Amelia understood why her mother was silent, and realized that her shoulders were shaking with small, silent sobs.

Grammy always came for a visit as soon as school was out, and Amelia had been looking forward to seeing her in just three days. She loved all of her grandparents, but Grammy was her special grandmother, the one who felt more like a best friend than an adult, the one who listened to her stories and shared her interests. Loosing Grammy was…unthinkable.

"No," was all she could say. She couldn't believe it. It couldn't be true. "No!" She shouted, standing up, and ran away.

Away from her mother's ragged crying sounds

Away from her father's calm grief.

Up to her room, where she slammed the door and dropped face down on her pillow and screamed until her throat hurt.

Then came tears. Hot, angry, frightened tears.

How could the world continue to exist if Grammy wasn't a part of it? How could she have woken up happy this morning if Grammy was gone?

It seemed like hours of crying. Eventually the tears stopped, leaving only dry, hiccoughing breaths to remind her that the world was heartless because it kept turning even though her life was ruined. There was a gaping hole where Grammy should be, but somehow things went on.

She lay there staring at the ceiling, her mind empty because thinking hurt too much. A sudden thud against her window drew her across the room, and she saw a bird sitting on her window sill, something in its beak, hitting it against the glass as if trying to break it open. A seed? She couldn't see it well enough to tell. As she turned away, she saw the candle they'd used the night before lying on its side on the floor where she'd left it.

Her thoughts wandered to last night, to Zed and his message...

She froze. Something tickled at the back of her mind.

She went over to her desk, pulled out paper and a pen, and wrote Zed's message down.

Rose—sorry – separation – little – 1 – love

"Little" and "1"—could they mean "Little One?" Grammy had called her that since she was a baby, it was her special nickname.

And the rose—that was Grammy's first name, *Rose.*

She took the paper and ran downstairs, finding her parents in their room.

"Mom! Dad! What time did Grammy die?" She demanded.

They looked at each other, then her father said, "It was about 4:00 yesterday afternoon, honey. Why?"

"The message!" She squealed and held out the paper. "It was Grammy!"

Her parents looked sadly at each other, and then turned doubtful looks on her.

"No, really, look!" She pointed at the words she'd written. "Zed's message was from Grammy to me! She even calls me "little one," see here?!" She pointed again. "I think this means something like, 'Sorry about having to go away' –you know, separation? —'Little One I love you.'" Amelia put the paper in her mother's hand and saw fresh tears welling up in her eyes. "Mom, don't you see? Grammy isn't gone! She's still out there—somewhere—and she came to say goodbye!"

8

UNBELIEVER

I don't believe in ghosts.

Myths. Stories. Pure fiction, meant to explain what we don't understand, or to scare us for entertainment, or even to sucker people into buying stuff or going to church or doing something else they otherwise would be too sensible to buy into.

Not me. Ghosts and fairies and supernatural beings and Bigfoot and aliens? Let the weak-minded, fearful, comfort-seeking masses believe what they want. Reality had everything I ever wanted, no need to go looking for more. No magic, supernatural powers, extra-terrestrials, or religion needed.

I also don't believe in true love or the existence of soul mates—or, for that matter, a soul. We're all just biological machines, wonders of physics and chemistry and evolution, random eruptions of chance in the great expanse of the Universe. We live until we don't. That's all.

So you can imagine my shock when I found out that I had died...and was still *there*.

It was just like they always show it in the movies: I was unconscious, in the hospital, and suddenly I was aware that I was floating over myself, looking down at the doctors working on me, my body lying there all broken and messy from the car accident. I watched for what felt like a long time. Then the doctors stopped rushing around and the machines in the room were all quiet.

I was dead. And I was looking down at myself, lying there, lifeless, with no idea what to do.

A doctor said the time of death out loud, then left the room. Various people were there, cleaning things up, unhooking my body from tubes and monitors. Someone pulled a sheet up over my face. But I was still floating there, looking down, wondering, *Okay, now what?*

I tried to look around, or up, or whatever, and see if there was some big white light or something. But no, there wasn't.

Eventually I left the room.

Movement isn't the same as it used to be. I found out that all I have to do is think a direction, a place, and I go there. So, when I wondered what was going on outside my room, I found myself moving into the hall. I followed my curiosity, wandering down corridors and into other rooms.

I was there for a long time. In the hospital. I didn't know what else to do, or where to go. I caught a glimpse, that first day, of my brother, who had been called by the hospital to come and deal with the situation, I guess. But something kept me from going to him, following him back into that room, with my dead body in it, from hanging around him or following him home.

It's not that I don't like my brother. He was fine, as brothers go. But we weren't close, in spite of being only a year apart, so similar in looks that everyone thought we were twins. We got along fine as kids, brothers who played together and all that, but kind of drifted apart after high school. I was pretty sure he'd be sad, but somehow I didn't think my death would rock his world. And there was no one else for me to check on; we were the only two kids in our family, our parents had been gone a few years already. Neither of us was married, and there was no extended family worth mentioning. So I let him do whatever he had to do alone and go his way.

I wished him well. I still do.

I stayed in that place for…it might've been years. I watched people. Stayed in rooms. It was a little like getting hooked on a soap opera sometimes: I'd happen across someone in their room, hear something about their condition, see an exchange between them and their family or friends, or doctor or nurse, and get interested. Then I'd just stay until it ended.

Plenty of times it ended with the person being discharged: happy ending. But there were deaths, too. And those were *really* interesting.

The first time I realized I was watching someone die, I paid close attention. I wanted to see if the same thing happened to them that had happened to me. Because I hadn't run across any other ghosts in all the time I'd been wandering around the place, so I wondered: is it only me? What happens when other people die?

So I watched. I was hungry to see it.

It turned out that each one was different. Sometimes—this is what happened that first time, in fact—there's just a movement, invisible like wind, that I could feel pulse through the room. Then the machines go silent, death is pronounced, and that's all there is. No ghost. Nothing.

But other times it's different. On about my fifth death I saw something that's exactly what I imagine my death must've looked like. There was a code blue—that means they're trying to revive a body that's trying to die. As the doctors were doing their business, a shimmer seemed to grow in the air above them. It developed a shape, and then I could see a person: it was the guy lying on the bed, but he was kind of there-not-there, transparent. Ghost-like.

When the machines went blank and the doctor called time of death, I watched the old guy floating there. He looked confused, and then a peace seemed to transform him, and he didn't look old any more, and he began to glow and fade at the same time. Then that wind—and he was gone.

I was jealous of every one of the deaths that ended that way. But I was also grateful because it could've been worse. I saw other kinds of deaths, and I was glad I'd escaped anything like that.

One time there was a young guy brought into the emergency room, where I visited now and then. He was a drug overdose case. He looked like he'd been living on the street, and it was a pretty short space from when he arrived to when they gave up on him. I stayed by his bed, though, because I was surprised: there hadn't been anything when he died. No wind, no figure, no sense of movement. Nothing.

I waited and watched.

After a while I noticed that something strange was going on with the body. At first, I couldn't tell what it was. Then I realized it was the ghost of the guy, but he was overlapping with the physical body so closely, it was like seeing a blurry form on the bed, not two distinct things. There was tension in the room; it seemed like the ghost was trying to get back into the body, to force itself back into existence.

It's not as if there was any flailing around, but it the atmosphere in there was uncomfortable, stressful. I thought it probably came from the desperate soul and what it was trying to do. The people in the beds on either side of the surrounding curtains started moaning in pain, I think because the spirit's frustration and anger affected them. The bad feeling in the room was getting stronger.

When I couldn't take it anymore, I moved closer and reached out to the guy.

"It's over," I said, or thought, or whatever it is that happens when I try to talk now. "Time to let go."

A ghostly head lifted away from the corpse, and for the first time since I'd died, *I was seen.* Our eyes locked, and after a moment of shock he screamed. Not a real sound—again, I'm not sure what happens when we ghosts try to make sounds—but something happened when he opened his mouth. The lights in the room flickered, a nearby person shrieked in what sounded like unbearable agony, and then it was as if the guy's spirit ripped itself to shreds. It seemed to be pulled apart like pieces of tissue paper, and the pieces writhed and darkened and became shadows—under the bed, behind the rolling cart, in the corner of the room. And even though I couldn't really feel anything anymore, it seemed to me like those shadows were colder than before, and maybe dangerous. I got out of there as fast as I could.

That wasn't the only time I saw a bad ending like that. But it got so I could tell when that was coming. Something in the air, in the room, something indefinable let me know. When I felt that, I got out.

But in all the deaths I saw, everyone who died went *somewhere*.

Except me.

I watched every death I could. I tried to keep track of patterns. I tried to figure out if there were rules to how things worked out—rules that maybe, somehow, had been broken when I died. If I could figure out how to fix it, then I could move on.

But time went on, and nothing changed.

One thing really stayed with me: the feeling of being seen by the drug overdose ghost. It was lonely being surrounded by people and never getting to be part of anything, not getting to participate, interact. I wanted it to happen again. Then one day, after another one of the good deaths had just wrapped up and I was wandering along the quiet, pre-dawn hallways of the maternity ward, it occurred to me: If I'm a ghost, I should be able to haunt people, and if I can haunt them, then I can be seen again!

I had no idea how to do it. Clearly, just floating around and being there wasn't doing the trick. I decided to see what would happen if I picked one person and followed them everywhere. Maybe that kind of focus would make a difference.

First, I picked a female nurse, but once I realized I'd have to follow her into the bathroom, I stopped. Next, I picked a young male orderly, one of the guys who does clean up and restocking and some janitorial stuff. I figured there was a good chance he'd be alone in some broom closet at some point, and maybe there I could make an appearance.

There are some funny, and a little embarrassing, stories I could tell about that guy, but they're beside the point. After about three months of being his shadow any time he was at the hospital, I gave up. It was no good, the living seemed to be oblivious.

Feeling incredibly low and hopeless, I found my way to the pediatric ward. Kids always cheered me up, even sick kids, because they were so sweet and imaginative and honest. I guess maybe it shouldn't have made me happy to be there, but it did, so that's where I went to drown my sorrows.

It was night, the lights were dim, and there weren't many people around. I went in and out of rooms, pausing here and there to read a chart or just look at a sleeping child. And then one of them woke up while I was in the room and *saw me*.

She was little, couldn't have been more than six years old. Her hair was black, and when she opened her eyes they were silver, like ice in moonlight. I froze when I realized she wasn't looking *through* me, she was looking *at* me.

"Hello," she said, sounding sleepy. "Are you a doctor?"

"No," I tried to speak, but she frowned and cocked her head slightly, like she couldn't hear me. I just shook my head no and smiled a little.

There was no conversation. She mumbled a few things after that, then fell back asleep. I stayed close, right by her bed—I couldn't wait for her to wake up again. The morning shift nurse bustled in around 5:00 am, and after checking various things she wrote in the chart "Fever broken" and the time. The parents arrived shortly after the sky grew light, and the little girl sat up and told them all about the dream she'd had of the strange man who had visited her, who smiled and stayed with her when it was dark, and she was scared.

I was still there, right beside her bed, but she didn't see me anymore.

You're thinking the same thing I am: she had a *fever*; maybe *fevers* were the key to being seen.

You can bet I haunted the infectious disease wing. And yes, people with fevers were more likely to see me. But fevers do funny things to you—you don't think straight, you don't know the difference between reality and fantasy, and even though it was great in the moment, when they came out of it, all they remembered—at best! —was a dream, a weird fever vision. I had no more reality to them than that.

It wasn't enough.

I racked my brains. I thought of every legend and myth and story I'd ever heard about ghosts. Who sees them? Why? What happens to them?

I tried everything I could think of: little kids, fevered or not—but mostly they weren't any different from the adults. There was one...but he died within an hour of seeing me, and the only difference was that when his little ghost appeared above his dying body, it looked down on itself, and then over at me, held my gaze for a few seconds, and then glowed its way into oblivion.

Also, it waved at me as it went.

Otherwise: no joy.

I was very depressed. I gave up trying. I'd stay in one place—a room, a hallway, a broom closet, an elevator, it didn't much matter to me— for weeks on end. Time lost meaning. I was aware of its passing only insofar as the things around me moved and changed. But for me there was nothing. I had only the hope that maybe one day I would fade into nothingness since there seemed to be no purpose for my existence. Maybe I was an oversight. Maybe I was a cosmic glitch and would eventually just wither away like an unused appendage.

It wasn't a great time for me.

Everything changed the day she walked into the emergency room.

Madame Josephina Electratoria was only there because her neighbor had collapsed on the sidewalk in front of her door, and she felt it was her duty to drive him to the hospital, thus clearing the way for her customers. She was dressed in grey sweatpants and a black sweater. I was existing by the front desk. She came in, helped her limping neighbor to a chair, and then came over to register him.

"He is Bernie MacMillan," she said briefly, handing some cards over to the nurse, "and I'm just dropping him off." She sounded annoyed and tapped her fingers impatiently on the counter.

"What is your relationship to the patient?" The nurse asked without looking up.

"I'm just his neighbor," she replied, "and I'm trying to be a good Samaritan, but I need to get going. Can't I leave him here with you now?"

"Ma'am we'll need you to stay with him until the triage nurse can see him," the nurse murmured, eyes glued to her screen, fingers tapping her keyboard and entering information from the man's cards.

"Great," she rolled her eyes. "How long will that take?"

"We can't be sure," the nurse's voice was flat as cardboard.

"Well, that's just wonderful," she said sarcastically. "Jesus H. Christ, no good deed goes unpunished, eh?" She smacked her hands down on the counter, and then said, "What's your problem?"

The nurse finally looked up. "Excuse me?"

But she wasn't looking at the nurse. Or talking to her.

She was looking at me.

"Well?" she demanded, leaning over the counter toward where I was. "Take a picture, it lasts longer!" She turned angrily and stomped back into the waiting area where her neighbor was slumped in his chair.

She'd seen me.

She was alive, and she'd seen me.

I followed her, stopping a few feet away, waiting for her to look over and see me again.

"Look," she said, not raising her eyes from the magazine she'd begun to page through angrily. "Whatever you want, I'm not interested. I'm leaving any minute, so get lost."

"I can't," I said. "I don't have any place to go. And you can see me."

I didn't expect her to answer. The little girl hadn't been able to hear me, why would this woman? But she did.

"Of course I can see you. And your homelessness is not my problem," she said.

I watched her, took her in. Her hair was curly and fell below her shoulders, streaks of an improbable red visible here and there. She had long fingernails painted red, and I could see signs that she'd washed heavy make-up off her face, especially around her eyes. Her voice was low and strong, and she moved like a person who was used to being in charge.

After a few minutes she sighed and looked up at me.

"What?" She demanded, but suddenly sucked in her breath and held very still. I saw her eyes dart over at the nurse behind the counter, and then back at me. Without looking, she reached a hand over to her neighbor, who seemed to be asleep in his chair, and patted his shoulder. He moved a little, made a noise, and resettled. "I can see you," she said at last, narrowing her eyes.

"Yes!" I said. "And you can hear me!"

"Yes," she spoke low, under her breath—I could tell she was making an effort not to be heard by the nurse now. Suddenly she rose from her chair and crossed back to the front desk. "Where are the restrooms?" She asked, and followed the nurse's pointing, looking over her shoulder at me and nodding her head for me to follow.

She didn't have to worry. I wasn't letting her out of my sight.

In the bathroom she checked under the stalls to make sure we were alone, and then turned on me. "You're dead," she said, hands on her hips, eyes narrowed.

"Yes."

"How long?"

"I don't really know," I admitted. "Quite a while, I think."

She started pacing. "Did you die here?"

"Yes."

"And you've been here...ever since?"

I just nodded.

She was quiet for a few seconds. "I guess that...most people don't see you around here, then?"

I told her about my attempts to haunt, my deathwatches. I told her she was the only one who had *heard* me, ever.

She listened, glancing at the door. "I've got to get back to Bernie. But you," she stepped right up to where I was—if I'd been alive, she'd have been right in my face, "are coming with me when I leave." She turned on her heel and went back to the waiting room.

I followed, waiting with her until her charge was taken to triage. Then I followed her out the doors.

It was strange because it wasn't. It had crossed my mind that perhaps if I left the hospital something different might happen to me. Maybe direct sunlight would do something, like it does in the vampire stories.

But no. I just followed her. She could still see me. I moved into her car with her, and moved with her car through the sunny morning. She explained things as she drove.

"I am Madame Josephina Electratoria," she began. "I am the only member of my family still in the family business: I'm a medium."

To say that this was a surreal experience is redundant, because pretty much everything since I'd died was surreal. But listening to her talk, I felt like I'd landed in some afterlife version of an Anne Rice novel: she came from a long line of female mediums, descended originally from gypsies. Only the women in her family had The Gift. She knew when she was only six years old that she had The Gift because her dead grandmother had come to her and told her so, so she grew up and set up shop and made her living communicating with the souls of the dearly departed for those left behind who had questions or unresolved issues. "I tell fortunes too, give Tarot readings, all that stuff—it's kind of expected," she added.

Problem was, after her grandmother, she'd never seen another soul.

"I'm good with people, I can read them really well," she said matter-of-factly. "It's not hard to be convincing. But I know the difference, even if they don't. And you're the first spirit I've seen since I was six."

We arrived at her place. I followed her inside. It was on a side street near a busy shopping area I remembered, and her professional rooms were downstairs while she lived above. True to the stereotypes, her "office" was draped in scarves, herbs and other witchy-looking stuff hanging from the ceiling. A stick of incense smoked on a small table in the corner, and the light was dim.

She led me through to the back, into a cheerful, bright kitchen, and sat down at the table.

"Stay with me," she said. "Let's see what we can do together."

"But what could I do? You're the only one who can see and hear me," I pointed out. "I won't help you convince your customers of anything." It wasn't that I didn't want to stay. She was interesting, this was something different, and I still felt a sense of elation at being seen by someone alive.

"Who knows?" She exclaimed, throwing her hands up in the air dramatically. "Maybe it won't make any difference, and you'll just be someone to talk to when I close up shop," she got up and poured herself a mug of coffee as she talked. "But maybe…just maybe you'll bring a whiff of the afterlife along with you; maybe other ghosts will sense you, and come calling when their loved-ones walk in."

I understood: she wanted to use me to do her job authentically.

Well, what else was there for me to do in this world? I agreed.

The first client was to arrive that afternoon. Josie (that's the name she told me to use outside of working hours) transformed herself from slovenly to mysterious, with dramatic makeup and clothes that said "gypsy" and "psychic," very exotic. The doorbell rang at 1:00, and Madame Josephina was ready.

I hovered in the room, mostly staying behind her, as she conducted the session.

It was a little old man who spoke with a thick accent, grieving for his dead wife. He wanted to communicate with her, just once more, and had come to Madame Josephina for help.

I watched as she went through her act. It was a good one, I had to admit. Exactly what you might expect, based on campy Hollywood movies and carnival sideshows, yet she brought a kind of gravitas that kept it from being demeaning or ridiculous. I kept an eye on the old man and the room in general, but nothing appeared, and although she gave me questioning looks periodically, I had to shake my head: no other ghosts showed up.

We kept at it, though, because she loved having a ghost to talk to, and I loved being able to talk, period. Neither of us minded too much that nothing more came of it.

But then one day, something did.

A teenaged girl came in. She didn't have an appointment and acted like she was afraid to be caught there. When Josie welcomed her inside, she closed the door quickly behind her, and went right to the silk-draped table in the center of the room. Josie cocked an eyebrow at me, and proceeded to her accustomed chair, sitting slowly as she asked, "How may I be of service, child?"

"It's my Mom," the girl said, leaning forward. "She died and," her eyes teared up and she wiped away tears as she spoke, "and I just miss her so much. I think," she sniffled loudly, "I've been thinking a lot, and I think I just need to know she's OK, and then I can..." Without finishing her sentence, she just looked beseechingly across the table, hope and sadness all mixed together in her face.

Josie smiled. "Of course," she said softly, placing a hand over one of the girl's hands, and then began her routine.

It began just as it always did, but when Josie got to the part where she chanted some old gypsy words she'd learned from her mother, the feeling in the room shifted. It felt like there was a fog rolling in. As I watched, it took on the form of a woman standing beside the girl.

"Josie!" I whispered. "Josie, do you see her? Standing there? Someone's here, Josie!"

"Spirits from beyond, although we cannot see you, please grant us the knowledge of your will and deliver your message," she said in a sing-song voice, telling me that she didn't see anything unusual.

I went around the table to the new ghost and tried talking to her.

"Hello," I began. "Are you here for— "

But she cut me off immediately.

"I don't have long," she moaned, wringing her spectral hands and looking down at her daughter with longing. "I've felt the pull ever since—ever since the hospital, but Janey," she reached forward as if to touch her daughter, but then pulled back, "I could tell she needed me, I had to stay."

I glanced over at Josie, and I could tell by the look of surprise that passed across her face that she was able to hear, if not see, our visitor.

"What do you want us to tell her?" I asked the ghost.

Josie covered by murmuring more foreign-sounding chants and rocking a little in her seat with her eyes closed. The girl watched her with an occasional tear falling down her cheek.

"I just want her to be happy," the mother said. "Tell her I'm all right, everything's good, and we'll be together again one day; but to live and be happy—I need her to be happy so I can go!"

Josie opened her eyes slowly and focused on the grieving teenager sitting across from her. She reached out and took both her hands.

"Your mother is with us," she said softly, and the girl gasped. "She has been with you all along, and she wants you to know it's all right. Everything's all right. She's going to a good place, but she needs you to be okay first."

"Mom?!" the girl sobbed.

"She loves you, Janey, and that will never leave you, but her spirit needs to move on."

The girl dropped her head into her arms and sobbed quietly for a minute or two, then sat up and took a few deep breaths. "All right," she said shakily. "OK, I can do that, I can be happy for her. Can you tell her for me?"

The moment the girl said those words, I felt that familiar stirring around me. The mother's spirit was going to move on.

"Tell her I love her," the ghost managed before she expanded into a serene glow and disappeared.

"She loves you, Janey," Madame Josephina said firmly, "and she has moved on."

Janey gave her a watery smile. Although her cheeks were still wet with tears, I thought she seemed lighter than when she'd come in. She tried to pay, but Josie refused. "No appointment, no charge," she said lightly. "Go buy yourself something pretty to wear, in honor of your mother, and we'll be even."

After she left, we lingered in the room in silence for a few minutes. Then I followed her back to the kitchen, where she sat down heavily in one of the chairs.

"I heard her go," Josie said, wonder in her voice. "I heard her talk to you, but then I heard the Spirit Wind take her away."

"Spirit wind?"

"Mama used to talk about it," she explained. "The breath of God carries souls to their next place in the Universe. She called it the Spirit Wind."

I told her I'd felt it and seen it happen lots of times in the hospital, but I never knew it had a name. I didn't say that I wished it would come for me and wondered why it left me behind.

Her eyes were sparkling. She stood up and walked over to where I was.

"Thank you," she said softly. "I was born to do this," her intensity had nothing to do with her gypsy act now, "and you have made it possible."

Business picked up pretty quickly. Word of mouth about that sort of thing works fast, and soon Josie was booked weeks ahead of time. It was nice for her. She raised her rates and saved money, she was able to spruce things up and started talking about moving to a nicer place. She could be more discerning, too; she had enough people coming to her that she could afford to give refunds if no ghost showed up for them—but most of those people wanted something for their visit and ended up getting Tarot readings or got their tea leaves read. She really didn't lose much.

But no-shows were more and more rare. It seemed like only people with real supernatural problems were drawn to us. Maybe they were compelled by their ghosts to seek us out? We'd talk in the evenings over our theories about how it all worked, but never really settled on one clear idea.

It felt good doing the work. Not only was it more interesting than my time in the hospital, but most of the time we were actually helping people. Sometimes it was like that first girl, and we were able to help someone find peace, end their suffering. Sometimes people came to us with questions they needed to have answered, and we helped them by being the go-between. There were even times when people came to us to end a haunting. They were plagued by a ghost who was better than I'd been at making itself known to the living, and they wanted to put an end to it. When that happened, it was usually the ghost who had unresolved issues, and once we helped them sort it out, they moved on.

I began wandering at night. Josie was working long days, going to bed early. I had gotten used to having things to do, now that I was working with her, and just existing in the dark, waiting for the next day, was depressing. So, I went out into the world. I wandered the city. It wasn't the same as working, but it was better than doing nothing.

It was interesting. I'd never seen this side of the things when I was alive. As a ghost I could go anywhere without fear, watch things up close that I'd never been a part of before. The lives of homeless people, for example. The crimes that only happen when the world is sleeping. The secret lives people lead after dark, their furtive, hidden acts, their desperation. Mostly I saw a lot of loneliness. That's probably why I kept doing it: I understood the isolation people created for themselves without realizing it. I, too, felt the gnawing misery of disconnection, and the quiet agony of helplessness in my inability to do anything about it.

Everything changed on one of these night time wanderings.

I was by the river, moving among the tents and sleeping bags of the homeless folk who sleep in the public park. Everything was quiet, and I was wondering if there were any other ways I could interact with the living world. As a ghost, could I access people's dreams? What if I tried merging with a living person? Would I possess them, like in horror movies? Could I read their minds? Would they know I was there?

A small noise jolted me away from my thoughts, and I followed it. It sounded like a kitten, but when I got closer I saw it was a tiny, old woman huddled under a bush. She was wrapped in something like a blanket, and nearby there was a shopping cart filled with plastic bags. Her breathing was shallow, and she was making a mewling sound. I realized she was afraid.

I could tell she was dying.

I stayed there, watching. After a few minutes she opened her eyes wide, and I experienced that thrill I always get when someone living sees me. She gasped, blinked, and then whispered, "Are you here to take me?"

I shook my head no, and smiled, trying to be reassuring.

"It's my time, it's my time, I know it, I can feel it," she said with her shallow breath, too quiet for anyone but me to hear. "You're my angel, you've come for me, lead me on, take me home."

She continued like that as the night wore on. The stars dimmed overhead, sunrise was coming, but I didn't want to leave her to die in fear. So, I stayed. I decided I'd wait, keep her company—who knew, but maybe I could actually help her go on her way, like she hoped?

Gradually, as morning greyed the shadows and the stars winked out, her breathing slowed down, her words stopped, and the spaces between breaths got longer and longer. But she did not close her eyes again. Her gaze held me without wavering. I was pretty sure by the time she took her last breath she wasn't afraid any more.

A hint of rose was reflecting in the quiet river when I felt the Spirit Wind rise. I watched her ghost glow into a faint, pearly essence above her tiny, lifeless body, and drew back a little to watch her go---I knew how this would end, and I was glad that she was having one of the nice kinds of deaths.

But as soon as I tried to move away, I felt a tug. She had reached out for my hand and was holding it, pulling me toward her.

"It's time to go," she said in a voice that was no longer old, tired, or fearful, but sweet and musical. "Come."

Me? Go with her? The Spirit Wind was never for me!

But this time it felt different. She was right: this time I felt it gathering me up, and I knew that if I let it, it would carry me on to...whatever is next.

But what is next?

And what about Josie?

I panicked. I pushed away as hard as I could, and she let me go. I watched a sad smile bloom across her glowing cheeks. Then the wind took her, and she was gone.

If I'd had a heart, it would have been racing. Joy, elation—I can move on! Fear, confusion—but if I do, where will I go? Regret, loss—what if that was my only chance, *ever*?

I told Josie all about it when she woke up. We had a full day of clients, so we couldn't talk about it much until after work. But that day there were two spirits that came seeking peace and release, and both times when the Spirit Wind came for them, I knew that I could have gone with them if I'd wanted to.

It was like each time it was an open door, where before there had been only a locked window.

By the time Josie sat down to her late dinner, I could tell her that it wasn't may last chance, and it seemed like I could go any time.

She ate in silence for a while, then asked, "What do you think did the trick?"

"What do you mean?"

"I mean, what made the Spirit Wind willing to take you along all of a sudden, when all this time it hasn't come for you?"

"I don't know," I said truthfully "Maybe it's because I helped that old lady."

"Maybe it's just...your time," Josie put her fork down and sighed. "I'm going to miss you."

But I haven't left yet. Now that I know I can, I want to make sure she's all right before I go—make sure her gift won't leave with me. We're trying some things. She got out her family Ouija board and is experimenting with using that to communicate with ghosts, without my help.

I'm sticking around, at least for a while. One of these days—I think I'll just know it's time—I will ride that *Breath of God* to whatever comes next. And even though I don't know what that is, I feel pretty sure that afterward, eventually, I'll see Josie again. Maybe then we'll understand all the things we've wondered about and laugh at how blind and stupid we were. But however it goes, I know I can leave, I'm finally free to go to something...*else*.

9

THE SKETCH ARTIST

"Look out, Tombstone!"

The locker door slammed, and someone shoved her from behind.

"Out of the way, goth girl, some of us are trying to get to class."

She heard several boys laughing but did not look up, choosing instead to stand still, hugging her backpack to her chest, looking down at the scuffed-up toes of her Doc Martens.

She would be late to math again.

"Just another day in paradise," she muttered, blowing her bangs out of her eyes and turning toward her classroom.

When the final bell rang, she wasted time at her locker, taking books in and out, rearranging them in her backpack, until the halls were empty. When she was reasonably sure most of the other kids were gone, she put all her school books back in the locker, shut the door, spun the lock, and headed out a side door.

It was hot and humid, and her black jeans and long-sleeved shirt made it worse. But Lori didn't care. She welcomed the feel of sweat beading across her forehead and trickling down her back. One more clear justification for her hatred of this town.

"Who would ever want to live someplace that's tropical in the middle of October?" she fumed, kicking pine cones as she walked.

There was a bus that she could ride home from the junior high. Since it was filled with the same kids who were doing everything they could to make her life miserable, she preferred to walk, even though it was three miles in this sweaty oven weather. She wouldn't get home until almost 5:30, but that wasn't really because of the distance. On her second day there—it only took one day of riding the bus to convince her she would never do that again—she discovered that the way home took her past a big, old cemetery. She decided to take a detour and explore it.

She'd gone there every day since.

Lori loved the silence, the absolute alone-ness of being surrounded by tall trees and tomb stones. It was a place she could be without worrying about what other people were thinking about her. And it was perfect for drawing.

Most days all she brought home from school was her sketch book and pencils. She got her homework done in class or during study hall, and she didn't really care about her grades anyway. Drawing was her passion. Ms. Denise, the art teacher at her old school, had encouraged her and shown her so much...but now all that was 3,000 miles away: friends, teachers, home. Thanks to her parents' divorce and her mom's new job, she was stuck in Williamsburg, Virginia, a small town which was, as far as she was concerned, full of hicks and idiots.

"But sweetie, there's history here!" her mother had enthused. "And it's all around us, every day---you can walk down to the colonial center any time and see historic interpreters in authentic clothing, just like they would've been 300 years ago! Isn't that cool?"

It was not cool. It was stupid—grown-ups dressing up, pretending they were people from the past? And all those layers of "authentic" clothing, in this weather? Who did that?!

Cool was fog sitting on the mountains all day, twisting its way into the valleys and through the city streets, even in the middle of summer. Cool was a school with so many different kinds of kids that no one thought being different was weird. Cool was the Castro and China Town and the Presidio. Cool was Muir Woods and Mt. Tamalpais hiking trails. Cool was U.C. Berkeley, where she dreamed of attending college eventually.

Cool was 3,000 miles away. This place was hot, muggy, and miserable.

But in the grave yard, at least it was quiet. She could let light and shapes and movement translate into pictures that flowed from her pencil. She drew what she saw around her, and it became beautiful. Trees, shrubs, grasses, beetles. Once she came across a snake sunbathing on a fallen gravestone. Another time, when she was sitting at the foot of a huge old tree, enjoying its deep shade, three deer came by, browsing on the grasses and leaves they found. She did her best to capture their grace on the page.

Many of her sketches included gravestones, naturally, and that's what had earned her the nickname at school. One of the jerks in her P.E. class had grabbed her sketchbook and flipped through it, showing his friends.

"She must live in a grave yard!" he cackled stupidly.

"Probably why she wears black all the time," his sidekick said. "She's like a one-person, permanent funeral!"

After that she kept her sketchbook in her locker during school, only bringing it out after the halls were empty and she was on her way home.

The cemetery was so enormous, she hadn't yet explored the whole thing. The day's heat being what it was, she decided to venture into what looked like an older section, further away from the road. There the trees were taller, their canopies thicker, the shade darker and, she hoped, cooler.

Settling herself up against the trunk of a massive oak (she could tell because of the acorns), Lori took out her sketch book, propped it on her knees, and looked around. Many of the graves here were a bit sunken, some of the headstones leaning drunkenly, their lettering obscured by lichen and moss. She watched a pair of squirrels play hide and seek. The leafy shadows on the ground looked like rippling water when the breeze stirred the branches.

There were lots of statues scattered around, everything from weeping angels and animals to actual people, which she guessed were supposed to represent the dearly departed. At first that's what she thought he was, another statue. He stood so still, and in the deep shadow of a tall pine, he looked like he was made of iron. When he moved she jumped, dropping her pencil.

"Hey—I didn't mean to startle you!"

Heart pounding and feeling foolish, Lori bent forward to pick up the pencil, hiding her face. "I thought you were a statue, that's all."

"Sorry about that." He tilted his head slightly and looked up, over hear head. "You found the best one here."

"Best one what?"

"Tree," he nodded at it. "I think it's about two hundred years old. It's my personal theory that every oak up and down Dog Street came from this tree's acorns." He grinned at her. She knew he was trying to make up for scaring her, and decided he was nice, even if his fashion sense was a little out of step.

"You go for the retro look, huh?"

"I gotta be me!" his grin widened. "Who wants to be like everyone else, you know?"

Boy, did she ever.

"I'm Alex," he walked to a nearby headstone and perched on top. "Do you come here often?"

She laughed, but decided he was all right. "I'm Lori, and you could say that." She wanted to explain more but wasn't sure where to begin. "Do you go to Whaley Middle School?"

He nodded. "Not my favorite place but at least I have Mr. Harvey for Social Studies. He almost makes the rest of it bearable."

"You mean Dr. Harvey? The principal?"

Alex looked confused for a moment, then shrugged. "Yeah, sure."

"I didn't know he taught classes. He seems cool. Maybe I can switch out of Ms. Swinson's class."

Alex was looking away from her. She liked how the sunlight peeking through the leaves overhead danced across his cheek. She was thinking about how she could draw that, capture it on paper, when he spoke again.

"What are you doing here? In the grave yard, I mean."

She flipped to a blank page and started moving her pencil in light strokes. "I like to sketch. I *don't* like being around other people—mostly," she smiled up at him, hoping she hadn't offended him. "This is the best place I've found to do both those things."

"Can I see?"

She froze.

Back home all of her friends had seen the things she worked on. It was just part of who she was, they all knew it, and it never felt risky to share with them. Here things were different. Art had been turned into a knife to cut her with, a label to brand her with, and she wasn't eager to give someone else a chance to do more of the same.

"Hey, it's okay," he was holding up his hands, palms facing her, and shaking his head. "I get it—art is personal. I didn't mean to invade your space or anything."

"How about if I work on some stuff, and show it to you when it's ready," she offered. She wanted to trust him, but…who knew what he was like at school, or who his friends were, or what he might say to them?

"Deal."

They sat in comfortable silence for a while, Alex watching the world around them while Lori let her pencil translate what she saw onto her paper. When her hand began to cramp, she put her pencil down and shook it.

"What about you? Do you come here often?"

His grin lifted the corners of his eyes. "You could say that," he echoed her own words. "It's beautiful. So peaceful. Right in the middle of the old town, really, but you can't hear cars or people or anything. I love watching the deer and the birds. And at night the racoons and owls—"

"You come here at night, too?" Lori was impressed.

"Oh, well, sometimes," he kicked his toe into the dirt and coughed. "It gets dark pretty early in the winter."

Lori suddenly remembered to check the time and moaned when she saw 4:55 on her phone screen.

"I've got to go," she said, cramming her things into her backpack and standing up. "I'm supposed to be home by 5:30." She rolled her eyes dramatically. "Mom thinks I go to the public library after school, to do homework. If I'm late, she might look for me there…"

"I get it," Alex stood up, too. "My mom can be a clingy sometimes, too."

Lori half turned away, but then looked over her shoulder at him. "Maybe, if we bump into each other here again, we can talk about … difficult parents?"

"Sure," his smile seemed to light up his face, and once again Lori wanted to drop everything and see if she could convey that glow using graphite and paper. "I'd like that."

She waved and began trotting back toward the gate, the sidewalk, and home.

It stayed summery through the entire month of October. Halloween felt more like Cinco de Mayo. Her mother encouraged her to dress up and go trick-or-treating in their new neighborhood ("It's a great way to get to know the neighbors, honey, and kids here do it well into high school—it's not like in the City, where all you had was a school dance! Isn't that cool?"). Instead, Lori shut herself in her room, turned out her lights, and went to sleep early.

It wasn't until the second week of November that the nights began to cool, and her long pants and sleeves stopped being so uncomfortable.

She would have been miserable if it weren't for Alex.

At first she'd been careful with him, like on that first day. But he always listened so intently—like a thirsty person drinking cold water on a hot day, she thought, soaking in every word she said. He never made fun of anything she told him. Eventually she'd told him everything: the divorce, the move, the bullying at school, the slow-burning hatred she felt for this town and everyone in it.

Well, almost everyone.

Alex told her things, too. He loved music. He'd taken piano since he was four years old, and his dream was to be a composer.

"Not like those old guys, the fancy classical music no one really likes," he'd said. "I mean, they're good of course, but I want to make music that goes with life."

"You mean pop songs?"

"No," he paused for a minute, looking at his hands quietly. "No, I mean the kind of music that makes you feel something, and then every time you remember it you have that feeling again. I want to write movie sound tracks."

"Really?"

"Sure! Think about it," he sat on the ground, legs crossed, and leaned forward eagerly. "Think about your favorite movie, the most important scene, and the music that goes with it."

"Like Harry Potter?"

"Exactly!" He beamed at her. "If you just listen to the music from the movies, you don't need the video part at all to feel exactly what each melody wants you to feel: scared, excited, happy, sad—it's all there in the music. Have you ever watched a movie without its sound track?" She shook her head no. "It's awful. You'd hate it. It's worse than naked. The music brings it to life---and that's what I want to do." He dropped his hands in his lap. Lori thought he sounded sad.

"That's amazing," she picked up her pencil and began to sketch the way a beam of watery sunlight seemed to give him a halo as he was sitting there, in front of the grave stone where they always met. He was so beautiful; she couldn't resist trying to draw him again and again. "You can do it, Alex. You'll be famous."

"You've never even heard me play," he still sounded sad, wistful, like he was talking to her from far away.

"Okay, so play for me then," she was working fast, afraid the light would fade, or he'd move his head.

"Sure. Some day."

She'd looked for him at school, but never saw him. Whaley Junior High was desperately over crowded. They were building a new junior high school across town, but until it was finished there were 900 kids crammed into a space built for 500, classes held in portables and conference rooms, with five different lunch periods because the cafeteria couldn't hold them all at once. So it wasn't that strange that she never managed to cross paths with him.

Part of her was relieved, anyway; what if he had friends who he had to be different with? In the grave yard she trusted him, she felt relaxed and like she could just be herself, and he was himself. School could change all that. She wasn't sure she really wanted to find him.

But at least three times a week they met in the old grove in the grave yard. They talked while she sketched. Sometimes she showed him what she'd been working on, sometimes he just let her work without asking to see it.

"What does your family do for Thanksgiving?" She asked him the week before the holiday. She wondered if the local people all dressed up like pilgrims or settlers or something.

"Nothing much. Just the usual dinner. How about you?"

"We have to drive up to New York to visit some relatives of my mom. I've never met them." She sighed. She had hoped she'd get to see her dad, but with only 4 days for the weekend, it wasn't enough time for her to fly to him or vice versa. "We'll leave Wednesday night, get back on Sunday."

"I'm sorry, Lori." She looked up to see him gazing at her, the look on his face so sorrowful and sympathetic, it almost made her cry.

"Whatever," she pretended to brush a leaf off the page she was drawing on. "I mean, you know, who cares? We'll go, we'll come back, it'll be over. Right?"

Alex just nodded.

"I'll miss you," he said quietly.

Lori felt herself blush. She'd been thinking the same thing, wishing she could stay and spend the holiday with him instead of going to visit family she didn't know or care about. Alex was her best friend.

"Well, look, why don't we text each other or something?" Why hadn't she thought of that before? They didn't have to wait for the grave yard—they could talk all the time, keep each other company where ever they went! "Technology to the rescue!" She held up her iPhone like a trophy.

"Nah," he shook his head. "I don't have one."

"What?!" She couldn't believe any kid didn't have their own phone. "Is it your mom? Is she one of those technophobe parents?"

"Pretty close," he said, and got up to wander a few feet away, his back to her.

Afraid she'd said the wrong thing, Lori followed him.

"Well look, it doesn't matter. We'll just look forward to coming here and telling each other about everything. Okay?"

He was still for a moment before shrugging his shoulders slightly. "Okay, Lori. That sounds good."

She tried to think of something to say but couldn't. She wanted to make him laugh, see him smile, and know that he wasn't upset with her.

"You'd better get going," he said without turning around, "it's getting late. See you later." And he walked away from her, his steps falling heavily, crunching in the leaves between the headstones. She watched until she couldn't see him anymore and worried all the way home.

Thanksgiving was over and Lori had gone back to the grave yard every day, as usual, on her way home from school.

Alex did not come.

The weather actually got cold, and she wondered if he'd gotten sick. Or maybe his over-protective mother wouldn't let him go outside when it was cold?

She fumed on his behalf, and waited in their grove every day, pacing around, too impatient to sketch. She had made a comic book lampooning her entire trip with her mother: the aggravating car ride, with endless traffic and too few rest stops; the cousins and their quirky personalities; the 200-year-old house made of stones where she'd been put in an attic bedroom on a cot that was lumpy and smelled like moth balls; the dinner disaster when the oven caught on fire and no one could find the fire extinguisher so the turkey burned up and they had to order takeout Chinese food; the old great-great-uncle who arrived a day late and wouldn't stop talking about magic spirits and the end of the world coming, who she'd thought was crazy until she finally realized he was drunk all the time. All the little details and funny, agonizing moments were in there. She had stayed up late at night working on it, fixing it, making it better, all for Alex.

She had imagined giving it to him, watching him read it and laugh, and seeing him happy, knowing he was glad she was his friend. 'And now,' she would say, 'let's go to your house and you can play something for me.' And from then on, they wouldn't have to meet in the grave yard, they could go over to each other's houses, like regular people, and it wouldn't matter what happened at school or anywhere else, they'd have each other and that would be enough.

But days passed, and no Alex.

The second week of December it snowed. Not more than an inch, just enough to be pretty, but not enough to shut school down. Lori was looking forward to seeing the grave yard in white, pushing back against disappointment with a hope that maybe Alex would come to see the snow, too.

She walked briskly on the slushy sidewalks. When she got there, she saw a set of foot prints in the snow leading toward the grove, and her heart beat faster. She patted her backpack, feeling the outline of the comic book next to her sketch book, already anticipating the look on his face when she gave it to him. She could see someone bent over the headstone in the middle and started running.

"Hey—" she called out, but stopped when the figure rose and turned to face her.

"Yes?" It was an old woman. She wore a dark blue winter coat that reached below her knees, and had a scarf wrapped around her neck. Her hair was silver, pulled back in a messy bun. She'd been crying.

"I thought," she started, then took a step backward and simply said, "I'm sorry." A bouquet was placed in front of the stone, fresh and fragrant: white and green and red against the lettering, a splash of color in the snow.

The woman smiled. "It's all right." She filled her lungs and tipped her head back, exhaling slowly, steam rising from her face. "I love the cold. I should come here more often, but it's easiest on days like this."

"I'm, uh, sorry for your loss," Lori tentatively raised a foot to take another step backward. She felt confused and wanted to get away.

"Ah, thank you," she said. "It was a long time ago, but..." she wiped her cheek and shrugged, "the pain never really leaves us. I think we just get used to it." She turned toward Lori. "Do you come here often?"

In spite of herself, Lori laughed when she heard Alex's words echoed by this stranger. "You could say that," she felt clever continuing the old conversation. "I kind of hang out here after school. I like the quiet."

"All by yourself? That sounds rather lonely." The woman sounded like she pitied her.

"I like being by myself," she snapped. "But my friend comes too, sometimes. We both like it here."

"Ah," the woman nodded. "Away from the durm and strang of the wide world, in a quiet place all your own."

Whatever, Lori thought, trying to figure out how get away quickly. Alex wasn't here. There was no point in staying.

"I had a place like that when I was your age," the woman continued, "in a park near my family's apartment. We lived near the panhandle of Golden Gate park, and there was a small gully with wizened old fruit trees left over from an orchard. I used to go there to get away from...things."

"Golden Gate park? You lived in San Francisco?"

"Yes. Do you know it?"

"Know it!" Lori forgot the cold. "I'm from there! We moved last summer. I went to a concert in the panhandle once."

Her voice must've given something away, because the woman nodded and said, "You miss it, don't you?" Not waiting for her to answer, she went on, "There's nothing really like it here."

"You can say that again." Lori rolled her eyes. "How long have you lived here?"

"A long time," she answered. Snow was falling again, and she shivered. "I'm afraid my old circulation isn't up to outdoor conversations in this weather. But my house isn't far," she hesitated, but then asked, "if you care to reminisce a bit, you're welcome to join me for a cup of tea before meeting your friend?"

Lori looked at her. She didn't seem strange. And her mother was always telling her she needed to make friends with the locals. Even if she was from San Francisco originally, she said she'd lived here a long time—didn't that make her a local?

"I don't think he's coming today," Lori finally said, hitching her back pack higher up on her shoulders. "Tea would be nice."

She followed the woman out of the grave yard. There was a neighborhood of older homes just across the road, and her house was the third one on the left. It was comfortable looking, Lori decided. Not fancy, just homey. Welcoming.

She entered behind the woman, following her through an entry way, down a hall and to the back of the house, where a kitchen opened into a cozy family room. Taking a seat at the table, she put down her backpack and waited.

"I'm Emma," the woman told her, "and please feel free to call me by my first name. I don't go in for the old-world formality much." She took their coats and lay them over a chair, then turned to fill a kettle, setting it on the stove top to boil. On the table she placed a tray with several different tea bag varieties, milk, and sugar. When the kettle whistled, she filled two mugs, brought them to the table, and sat opposite Lori.

"Tell me about yourself," she said.

She usually didn't like talking about herself, but something about Emma made her open up. She told her everything. It reminded her of talking to Alex—who she ended up talking about, too, including her confusion over why he'd stopped coming to meet her.

"And you don't have a phone number for him?"

Lori shook her head sadly. "I didn't think to ask for his home phone number when he told me he didn't have a cell phone. It was so stupid of me."

"Don't be too hard on yourself," Emma patted her hand. "There's likely a fine and reasonable explanation for his absence, and you'll both laugh about it together." She refilled her mug. "May I see the book you made for him? I do enjoy a good comic."

Lori thought she was just being nice but got it out anyway and handed it to her. She was secretly very proud of it and was glad to have someone to show it to. While Emma looked over its pages, Lori walked around the family room, looking at the knick-knacks on the tables, art on the walls. There were some unusual paintings, something between landscapes and the surrealist stuff her old art teacher had shown her, and Lori wanted to ask about them.

"This is quite remarkable," Emma said. Lori wondered if she meant it was bad and was trying to say so in a nice way. But when she looked, the silver head was still bent over the pages with interest, so she decided Emma meant it in a good way.

On a shelf at the far end of the room were several photographs, and she walked over for a closer look. The first was of a much younger Emma on a beach somewhere, holding a baby. She was smiling and the baby was asleep, gulls circling above them. The second picture showed her holding the hand of a little boy, maybe seven years old, both of them dressed formally—perhaps at a wedding? They looked happy.

Lori stepped over to see the next picture, gasped and dropped her mug.

"Oh my God!"

"Lori?" Emma stood up. "Are you all right?"

"Oh God—I'm sorry—" she bent to pick up the mug and pat uselessly at the wet spot on the rug where her tea had spilled. "I'm sorry, I didn't mean to—"

"It's all right," Emma brought a towel and handed it to her. When it was all cleaned up, she took the damp towel and turned back to the table. "What startled you?"

Pale and shaking, Lori went to her backpack and reached inside for her sketchbook.

"Alex and I used to meet three times a week, maybe four. We talked a lot, but I was always sketching. I drew him some of the time." She placed the sketchbook in front of Emma.

With questioning eyes, she opened the cover and began to turn the pages. At the third page she froze. She looked up at Lori, her face pale, then back at the page.

"This is your Alex," she said.

Lori nodded.

Emma put her hand over the sketches of Alex's face that Lori had made that first afternoon. She closed her eyes, then opened them and slowly continued to turn the pages, looking at every sketch, running her finger over the lines.

Lori remained standing, watching her, looking over at the third picture from time to time.

When Emma closed the sketchbook with a sigh, Lori said, "That was Alex's grave, wasn't it?"

Emma nodded.

Lori sat down heavily.

"So, I guess he's not coming back."

Emma looked up at her with eyes that were shiny with tears, but a smile on her face. "Perhaps not," she said, and she sounded calm, not like she was about to cry or freak out, Lori thought. "But maybe that's all right."

"What do you mean?" Lori felt like a small boat on a stormy sea, tossed between anger and grief, fear and wonder, awe and disbelief. How could this be real? How could they sit there calmly discussing him?

"He's been a friend to you when you needed one," Emma said slowly, absently rubbing the sketch book's cover. "And now, through you, he's shown me that he is not gone—he still *is*, somehow, somewhere, and every bit the boy I knew. The son I've missed."

Lori spoke slowly, frowning slightly. "So…maybe you'll see him again someday?"

Emma just nodded. "Maybe," she whispered. "Maybe we both will."

A clock chimed five times. Lori realized she was going to be late getting home, and it was already close to dark outside. "I have to go," she said, not really wanting to.

"Of course," Emma straightened in her chair, cleared her throat. "What would you say if I asked to keep your sketch book for a little while, and the comic you created? And then perhaps, in a day or two, you might come back for another cup of tea and get them back?"

Lori swallowed the lump that had formed in the back of her throat, feeling an overwhelming sense of relief. "I'd like that. Yes. Thank you."

She got her coat and they walked to the door together, but before opening it Emma wrapped her arms around her in a hug that caught Lori by surprise.

"No. Thank *you.*"

It was dark and cold. Ice was forming over the puddles of melted snow, and there was a dusting of fresh snow on the ground. Lori didn't notice the cold, or the time it took to walk home in the dark. Her thoughts were filled with Alex, questions and possibilities. She was also thinking about Emma, wanting to know more about her life—not just with Alex, but before that, her childhood in San Francisco, what had brought her here...*everything.*

By the time she got to the end of her block and could see her own porch light shining, she was smiling.

Now she had two friends, even if one of them was a ghost.

10

WAKING THE DEAD

"This is stupid."

"Sshhh, Daniel you don't want Serena to hear you!" His mother pushed him down to the end of the hall and put her hand on his shoulder, whispering. "I know this wasn't how you wanted to spend the long weekend, but we're the only family she's got. And family is important." She reached her other arm around his shoulders for a hug, but he shrugged her off and walked away.

"Whatever."

He refused to turn around when she whispered his name again, heard her sigh and bustle back to the bedroom with the dead body in it.

Great-great-great-Aunt Philomena, he reminded himself.

It didn't matter that he'd never heard of her, let alone met her, before the phone call last night notifying his parents of her death. Didn't matter that he'd had plans for the weekend, fun things to do with his friends that included a movie he'd been waiting to see. And pizza.

They all had to drop everything and spend the weekend with a dead old lady and her sister, in a house that smelled like wet dog and boiled cabbage and other things he didn't want to think about.

"It's called a wake," his father had explained. "In the old days it was very important to people. Aunt Serena said it was Philomena's dying wish to be waked by family, and that means us."

But the real reason his parents were doing this—Daniel had over-heard them talking after he was supposed to be in bed last night—was because of the Will. After her death, Aunt Philomena's entire estate would be left to whatever family members honored her last wishes.

"None of it will come to us as long as Serena is alive of course," he'd heard his father telling his mother, "but she's only two years younger than Aunt Phil was. How much longer can she last?"

And from the way they talked about it, Daniel could tell that the estate was worth a lot.

The whole thing disgusted him.

Mom, moving around with all this energy and excitement, trying to seem sad but barely hiding her happiness about the whole thing. Dad showing up for an hour or two to pay his respects, say hi to Serena, and then leaving to 'take care of some things,' which Daniel knew meant talking to the lawyer to make sure the inheritance would work out right.

Their hypocrisy was gross.

"Boy!"

He jumped. Aunt Serena had a way of making him feel edgy. She was standing in the doorway that led to the living room.

"Come help me while your mother watches."

"Why can't she help, too?" Daniel said as he followed her.

"She's watching," Serena's voice was high and had a whispery quality that made him want to lean closer to hear. "Someone must watch all the time or evil spirits might get in!"

"Oh," Daniel groaned, rolling his eyes. She meant *watching the body.* His dad had told him that there were a lot of traditions that had to be followed for a wake, but Daniel really hadn't been listening. He was too busy texting his friends to tell them he couldn't make it for their week-end plans. But he did remember him saying something about never leaving the dead person alone, to guard against evil spirits.

"Take this," Serena handed him a mound of what looked like black sheets.

"What's it for?" they were heavy and smelled like mothballs and dust.

"Mirrors," she spoke as if he were stupid, and he wished he'd paid a little better attention when his dad was talking.

"Why?"

She peered up at him, her tiny eyes black and bird-like, her head tilted as if she were trying to decide something. After a few seconds she laughed.

"I don't think you'd be asking your questions if you'd ever caught sight of a dead man's reflection and seen the invisible host of the dead marching forward to claim his soul!"

He followed her from room to room, handing her pieces of the black cloth for each mirror they came across. She was pretty creepy, but he knew old people could get senile and imagine stuff that wasn't real, so he wasn't buying into any of her superstitious stuff.

Where ever they found a clock, she instructed him to stop its hands, too. "Set them to 5:00," she whispered in her reedy voice.

"Why?"

But this she answered only with raised eyebrows and a shake of her head. She seemed to pity him, which made him feel stupid.

"Mom, why'd Aunt Serena make me stop the clocks?" He asked when he'd finally been able to escape the old woman to go find his mother. He didn't really like being in the room with a dead body, but at least the old woman lying on the bed couldn't laugh at him, treat him like an imbecile and make him do stupid things.

"Oh, probably as a way of honoring her time of death," was her answer. She was sitting in a chair in the corner of the room, reading a book.

"Doesn't this whole thing bother you?" Daniel demanded. "I mean, how can you just sit here and read?"

His mother looked up from her book and smiled. "This is all entirely natural, sweetheart. There's nothing to be afraid of, you know."

He rolled his eyes and shoved his hands in his pockets. "I'm not scared, Mom. It's just...creepy, that's all. And I think Aunt Serena has—"

"Juliette!" Serena was suddenly there, standing in the doorway, shrieking his mother's name. She jumped up from her chair, dropping her book.

"What's wrong, Serena?"

"The window, girl! The window!"

Daniel and his mother looked at each other, at the window, and back at each other again, at a loss.

Serena hissed and pointed with a crooked finger. "It must be open! So her soul can go free!"

Placing a hand over her heart and taking a deep breath, Daniel's mom smiled. "Of course. I'm sorry, Serena, I forgot." She crossed the room and pried open the old sash, propping it with the book she'd been reading.

"Good," Serena nodded, folding her arms. "Now you come with me. The boy can watch."

"Serena, I'm not sure—"

"Come!" the old woman had already turned and was making her way out of the room. "The boy can watch!"

Looking apologetically at Daniel, his mother said, "I'll be back as soon as I can. Just…hang tight?"

Daniel was alone with a dead body.

He stood at the foot of the bed just staring at it, unable to look away. He decided it looked more like a wax dummy than a real person. If he thought of it that way, it didn't seem so weird.

Something caught his eye to the left of the bed. When he looked, he saw that there was a mirror on the dresser there that they hadn't covered. In it he saw a bird reflected—it had hopped onto the window sill and was watching him.

Then he saw something else.

He could see the body on the bed there, too, and he swore he saw it move—the hand seemed to turn over, and there was a tremor across the face, the waxiness gone completely.

Impossible. It had to be a trick of the shadows and light. He was just spooked by that crazy old lady and her stories.

Quickly he grabbed the old afghan hanging over the arm of the chair and put it over the mirror anyway.

He could hear his heartbeat pounding in his head, and he went to the open window for some fresh air. The bird had flown away. The cool, fresh air of a spring day filled his lungs as he leaned out, resting his arms on the sill.

"No!" Serena was shrieking from the doorway. "Get away from the window, boy! Move! Move!"

Startled, Daniel jumped back, lost his footing and sat down hard on the bed. The sudden movement shook the mattress, and the dead woman's hand fell off her chest, where it had been placed, and onto his own.

As if she were holding his hand, the caress of death.

"Ahhhh!"

Daniel leaped up and ran out of the room, down the hall to the front of the house, out the front door and down the steps.

He didn't know this neighborhood, so he just sat down on the bottom step, feet on the sidewalk, panting like he'd just run a 6 minute mile.

He could still feel the cold touch of Aunt Philomena's hand.

Shuddering, Daniel cradled his head in his hands. This could not be worth it, no matter how much money the old lady had.

His dad pulled up ten minutes later.

"What's going on?" He asked with a friendly smile.

Daniel just gave him a dark look. "Mom's inside."

His father went in, then came back out a few minutes later. He sat down beside Daniel.

"Sorry about what happened," he said. "Your mother says you had to sit with Aunt Phil, and..."

"Yeah," Daniel cut him off, not wanting to go into it. "Whatever. When can we go home?"

His dad exhaled loudly. "Kiddo, we are staying the whole weekend. They'll pick her up tomorrow afternoon for the burial, according to her instructions, but we have to Wake her till then."

"Great," Daniel kicked the sidewalk. He picked up a piece of gravel and threw it as hard as he could. "Look, just don't make me be in that room again, okay?"

"I promise," his father stood up. "You want to come inside now?"

"I'll be in in a minute."

Daniel was eating a late afternoon snack in the kitchen when Serena found him.

"Boy," she made a 'come here' motion with her finger.

"Daniel," he said around a mouthful of crackers. "My name is Daniel."

Serena's face crinkled with a smile that showed missing teeth. "Daniel," she said. "Come."

He followed her to a room he hadn't seen before, because it had no clocks or mirrors. Just a twin bed and a wardrobe. And a lot of dust.

"You sleep here tonight."

"Okay," he said. "Thanks."

"Do you know why I yelled at you?"

If she was about to apologize, Daniel thought, this was a weird way to start. "No?"

"Everything we do has purpose," she held out her hands, fingers spread, and opened her arms wide. "People forget, but we must follow the ancient ways if we want peace."

More of her senior delusions, Daniel thought. But aloud he said, "Okay."

She shook her head. "No, not 'okay.' You don't know. In the Old Country everyone knew. Parents taught children the ways of things. Even here my gran taught me and 'Mena. But no one cares, and the young know nothing." Her voice tailed off and she shook her head sadly before she continued with a sigh. "The spirit must be free to move from one life to the next," she moved her hands in a way that seemed to be pushing air across the room, and Daniel thought he heard her joints pop. "The wind of the world draws out the soul and sets it free. This is why we open the window. But the living can get in the way—if you block the window, you block her way out. See?" She seemed to be genuinely smiling, and Daniel realized she was trying to be nice to him, even though she still seemed to think he was dumb.

"You thought I was blocking Aunt Philomena's way out?"

"You were."

"Well…I'm sorry? Do I need to do something about it? Can we just leave the window open for her, without me in the way?"

Serena shook her head sadly. "We cannot know. The time for a spirit's journey is a mystery to the living. This is why we watch, and why we open the window and stay out of the way."

Daniel was getting antsy. He didn't want to keep having this conversation, but also felt like he was supposed to do something.

"What happens if I, uh, blocked her?"

"You will know," Serena was backing away now, leaving him alone in the room. "You will see, you will know."

And then he was alone.

"Crazy," he mumbled to himself, and wished his parents hadn't made him leave his phone at home, "out of respect." He could really use a few hours of Netflix right now.

Lying in the small, lumpy bed that night, he couldn't fall asleep.

The house seemed filled with strange sounds. Every time he got drowsy and was about to nod off, something jerked him awake. Once he was pretty sure it was something from the kitchen, an appliance, maybe the refrigerator. Another time there was a low creek from inside the walls. Then he heard something above him, like a branch hitting the roof or an object being dropped in an upstairs room. He knew that was where Aunt Serena's bedroom was, as well as the spare room where Mom was sleeping.

He tried not to think about his father in a sleeping bag on the floor in the room with the dead body. Even at night, she still couldn't be left alone. Aunt Serena had insisted.

It wasn't scary, exactly. Just…weird. And creepy. Definitely weirdly creepy.

He rolled onto his side and punched the flat old pillow, trying to make it into something comfortable. From that angle he could see the window and the trees outside, a bright moon rising above the branches.

His eyelids grew heavier, and sleep settled over him.

He was dreaming when he felt it. Something cold. In the dream he thought it was ice: he was stuck in snow, trying to dig his way out. The cold seemed to move up his arm, slowly, with a tapping sensation, and that's what finally roused him. Eyes closed, still half dreaming, he reached with his other hand to brush at his cold hand. But he couldn't move it.

He opened his eyes and screamed.

Or he would have screamed, but he couldn't move, not even his mouth.

He was staring at Aunt Philomena. She was leaning over him, looking exactly as he'd seen her lying in her bed the day before. Except he was also looking through her, and instead of the waxy look of death, she was moving, eyes open and looking at him, mouth shaping words.

Her hand was holding his, the same one she'd touched before, and she seemed to be wringing it, patting it, trying to pull him out of bed.

There was nothing he could do. Movement was somehow impossible, he couldn't yell or make a sound, and even though he could see she was trying to tell him something, he couldn't hear what it was.

She grew more and more upset. He wanted to tell her he was sorry, he couldn't hear her, he didn't understand, but he still couldn't move. She frowned, and he thought maybe she was even crying—what do ghost tears look like, he wondered?

Then, with her free hand, she began pointing at the window. It reminded him of Aunt Serena yelling at his mother earlier that day, and then he thought he understood. Though he couldn't speak, his comprehension must've shown on his face, because suddenly Aunt Philomena stopped mouthing words, straightened up, and let go of his arm.

As soon as she let go, he knew he could move. He got out of bed and faced her.

"It's the window, right? You want me to open it? So you can be free?"

The ghostly face of his great-great-great-aunt smiled, and without bothering to be quiet, he ran to the window and pushed on the sash. It took a few tries before it would give way, and he ended up with cobwebs and dust on his hands and shoulder, but at last it was open wide. The night's chill spread through the room.

Daniel stepped aside. He wasn't going to get between the ghost and the window this time. He watched her turn to the window. She smiled again, closed her eyes, and extended her arms. Even as she stretched out she was fading, until nothing but a silver wisp of fog was left to be lifted out on the night breeze, rising and disappearing in the moonlight outside.

"Now you see, don't you?"

Daniel turned. Aunt Serena was standing in the dim hall just outside his door. She was wearing an old-fashioned night dress with some kind of cap, and he thought she looked like someone from the pages of a history book.

"You saw that?" He gasped, not sure he believed what had just happened.

Serena made a clicking sound with her tongue and nodded her head. "Mena has passed on. Tomorrow we will bury her. Get some sleep, boy."

Before getting back into bed, Daniel pulled the old afghan off the mirror and put it on top of his quilt. It was cold in the room now, but he didn't want to close the window. Maybe he'd dreamed it, but he wanted to hang on to the feeling he'd had when it seemed like Aunt Philomena's soul went past him on its way out the window.

He wasn't afraid. But he thought maybe, after all, Aunt Serena wasn't just some senile old woman with crazy ideas. He might ask her some questions in the morning.

11

WOMAN IN BROWN

November 9, 1857

She can't keep up. Her heart is beating too fast and her breath won't keep up.

"Run, to the river, run!" She is gasping out the words.

Ahead of her the sound of bare feet slapping mud—the river is close now. She can smell it.

But the dogs are gaining. She hears their bellowing hunting calls behind her, imagines the groaning leather as they strain at their leashes.

"Don't look back—just get across!"

The footfalls ahead slow.

"Mama?"

"Don't you stop, hear? I'll see you on the other side! Now *run!*"

She stumbles, falls. Ahead she hears running feet, then splashing, and knows Eliza is at the edge of the water.

She can make it now.

There are folk waiting on the other side. They'll help her.

The dogs are almost there.

Freedom. It will never be hers, but her daughter will have a chance now, and that is enough. She never could help the others, but Eliza— her last, her surprise when she thought she was done with all that—she is willing to trade her life to see this daughter escape.

She doesn't care what happens to herself, which is good because now her heart is going crazy, faster, and off beat. She sees spots in front of her eyes, and thinks she's back in the kitchen, feeling the warmth of the oven as she reaches in for a loaf of bread—the favorite of the family, special, reserved for holidays and fine guests, with her own combination of spices and oils folded right into the soft dough.

You must teach me your secret, Mistress told her, but she never really meant it. Kitchen work was for house slaves, not wives.

Too late now, anyhow, she laughs a little to herself. Didn't matter— nothing mattered but getting Eliza away to freedom, and she'd done that.

"I'll see you on the other side," she breathes out for the last time, and is already half gone when the first dog jumps on her, digging in with angry teeth.

July 12, 1963

"You have to go in and get her! You have to go back!"

The fire is so loud. It sounds like a storm around them, crashing down, obliterating everything.

"I had to drag *you* out—you think I'm going back in there?" He stomps away, fists balled, knuckles white. "What were you thinking? What were you *thinking?*"

She can't breathe, coughing and sobbing at the same time. Her words, though desperate, are slurred. "Go back and get her!"

There is no way to tell the difference between the red, flickering light of the fire, and the swirling red of the emergency vehicles.

Another siren wails, another truck arrives. Men are shouting. Sometimes other people's voices, their cries, rise above the noise.

She is keening now, rocking back and forth on her knees, coughing and wailing and crying.

"What were you thinking taking that stuff? You knew we had that baby for the night. What were you gonna do if she woke up and needed something? How were you gonna take care of her?"

"I knew you were there." She shuddered, the words a hoarse whisper. "I only wanted a little…. I only wanted to relax…"

Too disgusted for words, angry and terrified, he can only stare at her.

He feels guilt growing like a storm in his guts, and he wants to hit something.

Hot cinders blow, lightning rain. The air is on fire.

"Excuse me," a soft voice behind him. He turns. "I think this is yours?"

A little old man stands there, all bent over and dirty with smoke and soot, holding the baby. She looks bigger in his arms, but it's her, it's her.

"Ooooohhhhh my gooooood!!!" Keening turns to praise, but she still rocks on her knees, still can't stand on her own.

"You got her out," he can only say the obvious, but he reaches for the baby and thinks he's never felt this relieved in his life. Her heaviness is so alive, her smell more than smoke.

"Your daughter is all right, she's all right," the old man's face wrinkles in a smile and he pats the baby's head, now cradled in someone else's arms. "I saw…" he hesitates, "well, your door was open, so I went in to check as I was leaving, and there she was. So I brought her out—just in time, too, the fire got real bad, real fast." His eyes look behind the two of them, to the woman on the ground. He closes his mouth and nods his head. "That your wife?"

But he shakes his head no. "Girlfriend. This is her niece. We were babysitting, doing her sister a favor…" The baby coughs and he pats her back, raising her to his shoulder, not sure right now if he'll ever be able to let her go. Relief and adrenaline and fear and desperation wash over him.

The look on the old man's face as he glances behind him again makes him add, "She's having a bad night."

"Mmm-hmmm." He nodded over toward the ambulance. "Best take the little one over to the medics, get her checked out, just to be sure the smoke didn't cause any harm."

"Yeah," he says, and hurries away from the woman on the grass, the old man, the burning apartment building, precious cargo in his arms.

~

Samuel was awakened by the fire alarm, but it took him a few minutes to realize what was happening. By the time he was out of bed and in the hallway, the smoke was thick, and he was already coughing. Fast had left his body a long time ago, but he knew the way to the stairwell. He was only three stories up, so he wasn't too worried about getting out of the building in time.

The hall seemed longer than he remembered, though, and the smoke kept getting thicker. He thought he saw someone in front of him—a woman, he thought it was—her figure fading in and out of the billowing black air, and then she went into the last apartment before the exit. She left the door open behind her, so he followed her in, wanting to tell her to hurry, there wasn't much time.

"Hello? Ma'am? You need to come with me," he called out, but she didn't answer. He went through the rooms looking for her, but they were empty until the bedroom, where he found the baby. She was peacefully sleeping through all the noise. Feeling like he'd come for the purpose, he picked her up, turned and left. He didn't see the woman again, though he thought he could smell perfume even through all the smoke as he left the apartment, a spicy, cinnamon smell with a hint of oranges.

Eventually the fire was put out. Miraculously, no one had been hurt.

Samuel moved in with his son, his son's wife and their three children.

He wondered from time to time what ever happened to the baby girl he'd rescued, and her drug addict aunt (he'd seen it before, recognized the signs) and the boyfriend.

For the rest of his life, he was visited by dreams in which he was following a woman he could never quite see, one who seemed made of shadow and silence, wrapped in brown like smoke. He died quietly in the middle of the night two years after the fire, surrounded by the sleeping household of his son's family. They found him the next morning, a gentle smile on his face. Though no one else noticed, his youngest grandson could smell dim perfume, spicy and sweet, and he didn't feel sad because he knew it meant that Grandpa was some place good.

May 23, 1968

Grace loves their new house.

It's so different from the city where they used to live. Here there are trees and wild places, and even though mama keeps telling her they probably can't stay, she wishes on a star every night that they can.

The woods are filled with green light like pretty princess jewels winking and flashing from velvet shadows.

She feels no fear because how can a place so beautiful, filled with birds and baby dear and rabbits, be bad? She's seen the movies, she knows there's magic between the tree roots, in the hollows of the old, rotten logs, hiding under toadstools.

Mama doesn't usually let her be alone, but today Mama had to go somewhere, and Mrs. Gallagher from next door is watching her. She doesn't know about Mama's rules.

Deeper and deeper, moss and mud and scratchy leaves all around. She can still hear cars. But in her mind, she is far away in a magic place, and all she wants to do is find the fairies, talk to the squirrels, kiss the magic frog.

A perfect hollow log. Moss on top, mushrooms growing on it, half-buried in old leaves. The gateway to Fairy Land!

Her shoulders won't fit inside, but she's sure if she can just reach far enough, she'll feel the door, the fairies will let her in, and—

OUCH!

Fire shoots through her hand—it won't stop, won't let go!

She scrambles back, and sees the big snake attached to the soft skin between her thumb and hand. She screams, wordless shrieks of pain and fear. Where are the fairies? Why aren't they helping her?

The snake is moving, waggling, and finally lets go and like lightning, is gone. Her hand hurts. She doesn't see blood, but feels a tightening, her fingers are getting big like a balloon, and she feels dizzy.

She lies on the damp, soft ground, crying. The sky above her seems to be moving, blurry, fuzzy, and she is scared.

Which way is home?

Sit up.

She stops crying, listens.

Sit up, now. Put your hand up in the air.

Sniffling, she does what the voice says.

Now keep it there, no matter how tired your arm feels.

She nods, though she doesn't understand why she must do this.

Good girl. Now be still.

She feels a little breeze tickle the hair on the back of her neck, and it cools her, even though she's feeling hotter and her head hurts. Slowly she turns her head to look around and see the lady who's telling her what to do, but can't find anyone. She thinks for a minute that someone tall is standing just behind her, but when she turns her eyes to see there's no one there.

She's a good girl. She waits. But her arm is getting heavy and her brain feels like it's spinning inside her head.

Not long, now. Keep your arm up.

She whimpers a little. This is hard. She wants Mama to come and make it stop hurting, make her head hold still.

The woods seem to be getting dark around the edges. She squints up toward the sun to see why it's going away, but has trouble moving her head backward, so gives up. Things get darker. She can see the lady now, and she is tall, wearing a long brown dress that sounds like rustling bushes when she moves.

The rustling gets louder and louder and then she hears barking, and there's a dog. It's barking right at her, but she's a good girl, she won't run, she won't put her arm down, the lady said to stay like that.

It's so dark now she almost can't see the person who runs through the bushes and grabs the dog's leash.

"There you are! Bad dog---Oh my God! Little girl, are you okay?" The person is bending down and looking in her face, but she can't really see him, and she only hears his voice from far away. Maybe she's going to live with the Fairies after all?

She wakes up in a bed. Mama is sleeping in a chair nearby. It's dark and quiet, but her brain isn't spinning anymore, so she knows everything is all right. Her hand where the snake bit her is wrapped in white bandages, and it doesn't hurt any more.

She hears a soft sound almost like wind in leaves and looks across the room to where a curtain is hanging. The shadows behind it are dark. She thinks she sees a tall woman there, but sleep is making her eyes fall closed and she's not sure. As she drifts off, she's glad that Mama took her to a place that smells so nice, cinnamon and oranges are two of her favorites.

February 4, 1986

"Grace, you're such a worry-wart!"

"I am not getting in that car with you behind the wheel. You're drunk, and I am not gonna let you drive!"

"Ugh, fine!" Eyes roll, stumble walk to the passenger side, fumble with the door, get in. "Here, take the keys."

Grace's night is ruined. It was all fun until Ashley went overboard. Trying to drink hot guys under the table is never a good idea.

Grab the keys, start the car. "Get your seatbelt on, Ash."

Eyes rolled so hard she can hear them rattling. The click of the seatbelt buckle.

Angry silence as the wet road sluices by under their tires.

"I don't know why you always have to ruin my good times…" head lolling to the side, Ashley's words are slurred. Grace already knows she won't remember this tomorrow, doesn't bother to answer.

Something flashes across the headlights just before she feels the impact slam into the car. The wheel yanks out of her hands, the car is spinning. She realizes the airbags have deployed, and looks at her mirrors, out the windows, trying to see what's happening.

Something in the back seat—eyes? —but no, nothing.

The car slams into something else and stops moving. Her head went sideways into the door, but she's still conscious. Ashley is bleeding, un-conscious, but whether it's from impact or alcohol Grace can't tell.

Suddenly Ashley screams.

"Help! Oh my god, Help! I can't feel my legs! Help me!" Weak thrashing, arm tangled in the deflated airbag.

Grace notices the burnt smell like gunpowder from the airbags, and something else: it reminds her of Christmas, oranges and cinnamon and…

Eyes flash, deep brown like chocolate, then they're gone.

Grace smiles and lays her head back. "It's all right, Ashley. We're safe," she croons this again and again until her friend is still, and sirens in the distance tell her it's true.

December 11, 1994

"Mama, where we going?"

"It's a short cut, baby." *Better not to walk through the park after dark.*

"It doesn't feel short."

"Come on now," *please don't whine at me after the day I've had.* "It's like going on an adventure, right?"

"But it's so dark, I can't see anything!"

Count to ten. Do not get mad. It's not her fault Ty forgot it was his turn for pick-up on the same day your car decided to break down.

"I thought Daddy was gonna get me today. You said you had to work."

"I thought so, too, baby, but sometimes things change. Now come on, Tahnie—we'll hurry home and get nice and warm, and you'll see Daddy next week."

"But I don't wanna see Daddy next week! Why can't he just come home and live with us again?"

One, two, three, four, five...

Puddles throw streetlight back up into their faces, everything is slick and black from rain.

"We're almost home," *thank God, just two more blocks after this cut-through alley.*

"Mama?"

A lurch in her step, she feels the little girl slip and stumble.

"Mama!" her question becomes a shriek.

"Shut up." Muffled voice, masked face, dark clothes—*he's holding onto my baby!*

"No!" without thinking she screams.

"I said SHUT UP!" he jerks on the little arm so Tahnie whimpers and waives his other hand in her face. He's holding a gun, black and hard and powerful. "Throw down your bag and keep the kid quiet."

Grace looks at her daughter, who's biting her bottom lip and has tears slipping down her cheeks. "Baby, we're gonna be fine. Don't be scared, and don't make a noise. I'm putting my bag down. Take whatever you want, just don't hurt us," she tries to make eye contact with him, but his eyes are empty slits, all rage and venom.

"Get away from the bag. Take the girl. Now both of you lie down— face down! Don't look at me!"

She feels the kick on her thigh, and another one to her ribs, but they don't hurt. All that matters is that Tahnie is on the other side of her, she's safe, she's staying quiet.

She can hear him rummaging through her bag. It's her work back pack, filled with all her daily things: a clean shirt, extra set of scrubs, keys, make-up, hair things. Her wallet is in there, too, and her phone, and he cackles when he finds them.

Beside her, Tahnie starts whimpering.

"Ssh, baby, stay brave now. Keep quiet. Everything's okay."

But she gets louder.

"I said keep her quiet." Another kick to her ribs. She doesn't feel it now, but she knows it's going to hurt later.

More rustling. *What's he looking for now?*

The sound of wind.

"What the f—" she hears him drop her bag. His feet scuttle back and forth a minute. "What are you trying to pull?"

Another kick. The impact jolts through her whole body, and Tahnie feels it too. She sobs loudly.

"Ssshhh, it's okay, it's okay…"

Wind blows over them. It smells clean. *If we get out of this, I am leaving the city forever,* she thinks. *I am taking Tahnie to where the air is clean, and there aren't any dark alley punks.*

"Hey!" he bellows. His feet scuff against the wet pavement. Tahnie has gone quiet at last.

Suddenly he cries out, as if he's hurt, and she hears the gun drop—it goes off—she screams, flailing sideways to shield that tiny, fragile body.

The world seems frozen.

Then little hands patting her, warm and safe and whole.

"It's all right Mama," Grace can even hear a smile on her daughter's face. "It's okay. We're safe."

She lies there a few minutes, listening with every part of herself. There is no sound. Finally, she lifts her head and looks behind.

On the sidewalk, half soaked in puddle muck, her things are scattered around. All of them are there. Even her wallet and phone. A few feet away she sees the flinty shape of the gun, lying in the street where it fell.

No sign of him.

Fast as she can, she shoves everything into her bag, grabs Tahnie's hand, and begins walking. It's all she can do not to run, but she knows the little girl couldn't keep up, so she holds back.

In five minutes they are home.

Her hands shaking, she does the necessary things: cleans her face and hands, checks Tahnie for injuries, changes clothes. She pulls something out of the fridge and heats it in the microwave—doesn't even know what it is until Tahnie's happy exclamation of, "Mac 'n Cheese!" Sets the table and dishes it up.

"Mama, you eat, too," she is watching with big eyes. Grace wills herself to take bites, chew, and swallow.

After dinner she puts Tahnie to bed.

"Early bed time, baby, it's been a long one for both of us."

Sitting on her bed, saying good night.

"Mama, what happened to the bad guy?"

"Honey, I don't know, and I don't care. We got away and that's all that matters."

"But he wasn't going to hurt us."

"How do you know?"

"I was scared at first, but then I knew we were going to be okay."

Grace frowns. "Honey, how did you know?"

"When that wind blew Christmas over us, I knew we'd be all right."

"Blew Christmas? Tahnie, what are you talking about?"

"Didn't you smell it, Mama? It was the Christmas bread you always make, that's all sweet and spicy and tastes like oranges. When I smelled that, I knew we were safe."

She stared at her daughter. Forced a smile. "Good night, sweetheart. Sleep tight."

April 10, 2024

James was annoyed. Why his mother loved this dive was beyond him. It had been her favorite place, though, so every Sunday he brought her here for their weekly brunch.

They never got his order right. And he often had to ask to be reseated two or three times before he could find a comfortable chair at a table that wasn't in an obnoxious location.

Sometimes he thought they sat them at that little two-person table that wobbled, right next to the bathrooms, on purpose. Just to see what he'd do.

They should show more respect for an elderly woman and a man such as himself.

It seemed even worse than usual today. He had to wait 35 minutes for a table, though he watched other groups walk right in.

"They called ahead, sir," the cheeky little hostess told him when he complained.

He was finally seated at something more the size of a lap tray than a real table. It was shoved up against the wall in the back corner, between a large potted tree and the doors leading to the kitchen.

"Outrageous!" He fumes at the waiter who comes to fill his water glass and hand him a menu. "You can't seriously expect me to sit here?"

"I'm sorry sir." Was the man's tone mocking? "This is the only available table right now. If you prefer to wait in the lobby…"

"I've already been waiting almost an hour!"

"Yes sir, on holiday weekends like this we tend to be fully booked."

James snatches the menu out of his hands.

His mother had always ordered the same thing: oatmeal with fruit, cream, and maple syrup.

"You could make that for yourself at home, Mother," he'd pointed out each week. "Why come *here* and order it?"

She always smiled and shook her head. "James, sometimes its nice to have someone else do the normal little things for you. I don't want fancy," she raised her eyebrows and he knew she was implying that he was too fussy. She always managed to make him feel too demanding. "Just simple and plain, but...once a week I like to let *them* do the cooking."

He orders the eggs benedict with hollandaise on the side---that way, which ever part of the dish they ruin, he could reorder while the rest remained intact with him at the table.

"These eggs are overdone," he informs the waiter twenty minutes later, "and the hollandaise is separating. Take it away and bring me another."

Without an apology the man takes away his dishes, leaving him with only his ice water, though all the ice has melted. No one has come by to offer him coffee. It took far too long for his food to arrive. On every level, today's experience here is the worst it has ever been.

"I hope you're happy, Mother," he mutters.

He had assumed that, after her passing six months ago, he would never return to this place. He'd only come each week for her sake. Yet week after week, at 10:00 on Sunday, he found himself waiting for a table, anticipating the poor service, demanding better tables, and critiquing his meal to the maître d' on his way out.

I suppose it's simply become a habit, he has told himself. Today makes him decide it is a habit he must break.

Another ten minutes passes, and the waiter does not reappear. His water glass is empty. He scowls around the room, searching for someone to flag down. There seems to be a great deal of commotion a few tables away. He looks more closely.

Two other diners are causing a problem. He sees a silver-haired woman sitting with someone younger—he guesses it's her daughter. The younger woman is out of her chair, waving her arms and crying out about something, but he can't hear her words. The older woman looks ill, slumped in her chair and very still.

Now they've poisoned someone, he thinks with satisfaction. *They deserve to be shut down—this place is execrable!*

Several people have rushed over by now and he can't see what's happening—the tree is in the way, and he isn't going to give himself a stiff neck twisting around to watch. The kitchen doors burst open and others run in. Then, just as he's made up his mind to simply walk out, he smells something delicious.

James leans forward, nose toward the kitchen doors.

Citrus and spices—vanilla? Cinnamon?

He glances down at the menu but sees nothing that could fit that description. Perhaps it is a daily special the waiter has neglected to tell him about. It wouldn't be the first time.

Resettling in his chair, James glances over his shoulder. The fuss with the two women has settled down. Both of them are still there, smiling now and being fawned over by several of the staff—meanwhile here he sits, completely ignored.

Typical.

Instead of walking out, however, he makes up his mind to tell the waiter to forget the eggs benedict and bring him whatever *that* was. Its perfume was ambrosial, heavenly. He thinks perhaps his mother would have given up her oatmeal, even, to have some.

October 21, 2056

The daylight is fading. Grace watches the colors in the clouds dim until those glorious, fiery pinks and oranges are nothing but shades of gray. A single star pulses right at the top of the sky.

"Good night, Mama," Tahnie comes in with a small tray. On it are a glass of water, her night time pills, and a piece of chocolate.

Grace smiles.

"Everyone else asleep?"

Her daughter nods. "You know me. I'm like you. I like to stay up and feel the peace of the house when there's nothing but quiet."

"We've always been a couple of night owls," Grace turns back to the window and sees black night outside, a sky full of stars now. She doesn't remember night falling, thought it had just been sunset. But time is funny like that these days, and she is learning to accept it.

Tahnie bends over to place the tray on her bedside table and kiss her cheek. "Those babies wake up early, though, so we ought to be going to sleep, too."

The house was full of family this summer. Tahnie came every year for a week or two, but this year she'd arranged a big gathering: Jerome was there, freshly retired. He'd taken on her garden and turned it into a glorious and fruitful plot of wild flowers and vegetables.

"My grandparents were sharecroppers before they left the South," he told anyone who complimented his work. "I guess some of that came down to me."

All three of their children were here, too. Renee, whose summer project of bee keeping complimented her father's gardening efforts. Her wife Tillie made sure there were fresh flowers in every room. Basco and his wife and their twins, Grace's first great-grand-babies, had arrived a week ago. And Tony and Lola came up from the city too. They couldn't afford to leave their fledgling restaurant during the week, but they both came for the weekends. They arrived with good news, announcing that Lola was pregnant—finally, after ten years of trying. Their joy was contagious.

The moon is up now, casting long shadows because it's full. In its pearly light Grace feels young, and she reaches up, touching her own cheeks to make sure.

Behind her, from the dark corner where moonlight can't reach, she hears the stirring of air. A sound of movement, soft and silken.

Grace smiles.

"I thought I might be seeing you…one last time."

A lovely, warm perfume fills the room, mingling with moonlight and starshine. Grace feels gravity loosen its hold on her, and shivers.

"When I'm gone, will you keep watch over them? All of them? Like you did for me?"

There is a flourish, like long skirts swishing, and Grace can see the shadows coming together in a tall shape, all in brown, eyes that watch and smile.

She lets out her breath and feels herself rise into the diamond sky.

12

THE LAST FAREWELL

Sam loved Frodo.

On weekends and vacations, they were inseparable: a boy and his dog gamboling through summer days, hot and humid and filled with dusty adventures by day, firefly studded camp-outs by night; autumn leaf piles raked up and jumped in and raked up again, foraging for kindling and stacking firewood and playing fetch with the smaller sticks; spring time jaunts through the woods behind the house, a treasure trove of steep-banked creeks filled with fish spawn and tadpoles, nesting birds and mud holes.

Sam was only one year old when the family rescued the funny-looking puppy with a broken leg. Someone had thrown him from a passing car in front of them, and Mrs. Hardin had screamed at her husband to pull over so they could save the whimpering mutt.

They learned to walk together. Mr. and Mrs. Hardin named him Frodo because of his devotion to their little baby, whose nickname was "Samwise." The pup cried at night unless allowed to sleep beneath the baby's crib, and later at the foot of his bed. Whenever the family left the house, they returned to find Sam lying on the floor of the foyer, nose touching the bottom of the door, tail wagging like a propeller at the return of his people---but it was Sam who got the face-licking, and whose every step he followed, a furry shadow.

It was a dark day when Sam went off to Kindergarten. For the entire seven hours that he was gone, Frodo waited at the door, whining. Mrs. Hardin could not tempt him away with food or water, not even left-over steak from last night's dinner, which he had begged for shamelessly until Mr. Hardin banned him from the dining room.

Mrs. Hardin put Frodo on a leash and took him with her as she walked down to meet her little boy at the bus stop after his first day of school. Sam emerged from the bus with tear-streaked cheeks, hurtling himself onto his beloved Frodo, sobbing, "I missed you so much, boy! I missed you so much!"

That night at dinner, Sam informed his parents that he would not be going back to school unless Frodo could go, too. It took some very stern reasoning, and not a few promises involving ice cream, to convince him that he *would* go...and his mother helped by presenting him with a notebook to take with him. "Any time you miss Frodo," she suggested, "Take this out and draw a picture of what you're doing so you can remember to tell him about it when you get home. It'll be like having him there with you," she smiled at the watery eyed solemnity with which her little boy accepted the notebook, showing it to Frodo and explaining the idea to him before placing it in his little backpack.

Every day from then on, the first thing Sam did when he got home from school was take out the notebook. He'd sit down with his dog, turning the pages and bringing his best friend up to date on his doings. Kindergarten alone filled five of the spiral notebooks, and though drawings changed to notes as he grew older, Sam kept the habit up, while his mother kept the used notebooks on a shelf in the garage, thinking one day they would be a wonderful keepsake for him.

Frodo grew accustomed to the daily absences. He was eventually willing to leave his post at the front door for food, water, the occasional visit to the back yard. If Mr. or Mrs. Hardin were home sick, he would sit with them, or lie at their bedroom door as they slept. But his inner clock never failed to alert him when Sam was due home, and he was always waiting at the door when Sam turned the nob.

In 6th grade, Sam was allowed to ride his bike to school. The middle school was closer than the elementary school had been, less than a mile away, and so long as he wore a helmet and promised to follow the rules of the road, his parents let him take this small step toward independence. The first morning of the year he mounted his bicycle, whooping for joy and standing on his pedals as he wheeled down the driveway and into the road, not noticing that he'd neglected to close the side door. He heard Frodo before he saw him, barking and loping along behind him, just as they'd done all summer long, exploring neighborhood streets and the long, dirt farm roads beyond the woods that led to the river where they'd fished and napped and played fetch, digging in the sand for pirate treasure, sharks' teeth, and native artifacts.

"Go home, boy!" He shouted over his shoulder, but Frodo ignored him.

At school, Sam locked his bike up and bent over to take Frodo by his two ears, a gesture that meant *pay attention, now, I mean it.* "You've got to go home, boy," he said firmly. "I can't take you back because I'll be late for the first day. Go home." He pointed back in the direction of the house, but Frodo merely sat down and panted quietly, letting his tongue hang out, grinning.

Sam had no choice but to leave him there. Several of his classrooms had windows looking out on the playground where the bike racks were located, and every chance he got he looked to see if Frodo was still there. Every time he looked, he saw a mottled furry shape sitting or lying down next to his bike. When the final bell of the day rang, Sam ran to his bike and hugged Frodo.

Back home, Mrs. Hardin had been beside herself worrying about what she would tell Sam. She knew it would break his heart to lose the dog. She'd driven around the neighborhood for hours, even driven to the local pound and checked to see if he'd been picked up. She had to sit down and cover her mouth with her hand when she saw Sam walk in with Frodo at his heels, both of them smiling.

"Guess what Frodo did today, Mom!"

From then on, when the weather was good, Frodo went to school with Sam, waiting for him all day. He became popular with the other kids, and at recess they fed him treats they'd snuck out of the cafeteria, so Sam wasn't worried too much about Frodo going hungry. When it rained, or got too cold, Mrs. Hardin insisted on keeping Frodo at home. On those days he reverted to his old habits, waiting at the door for his best friend to come home.

One foggy morning in spring, Mrs. Hardin had a difficult time keeping Frodo from following Sam. It was wet, more rain was predicted for the early afternoon, and she didn't think it was a good day for him to follow along. She also made Sam strap a headlamp onto his helmet and wear a yellow reflective vest over his coat. Although he stayed on quiet, neighborhood streets for the whole trek to school, she still worried about his safety. When there was fog, she was not willing for him to take chances. Sam rolled his eyes and argued.

"It's this or walk, young man," was all she had to say. Sam strapped on the light, shrugged into the vest, and was out the door.

Frodo lunged after him, but she grabbed his collar just in time. "Not today, old boy," she grunted, pulling him back and closing the door. A low growl rumbled in his throat, and Mrs. Hardin let go of his collar in surprise. He'd never shown the slightest inclination at violence, never growled at one of the family before. She shook her head and worried. She'd heard of dogs getting senile and turning on their families in old age. She hoped this wasn't the beginning of something like that. Frodo was almost twelve years old, after all.

Frodo merely lowered himself to the floor, placing his nose at the corner, and whined.

Sam was eager to get home that afternoon. It was drizzling, but no longer foggy. He had a lot of homework, but first he wanted to show Frodo the new game they'd learned in Gym class. It was a two-person version of Four-Square that he thought he might be able to teach Frodo to play if he used a tennis ball, rather than the large rubber balls in the gym. Frodo had always been a smart dog, quick to learn tricks, and wouldn't it be fun to show the other kids that his dog could play the game at recess?

He was halfway home when he realized he'd forgotten to put on the vest his mom had made him wear that morning. *Oh well*, he thought, *it's not foggy now. I'll just tell her I forgot, and I'll get it tomorrow.*

Suddenly a screeching sound caught his attention, and he swerved out into the road as an SUV peeled out of a driveway, clearly not having seen him. He recognized the car—it was his friend Ben's mom, probably late to pick up Ben's little sister from the elementary school. Ben complained a lot about how his mom was always late and had been even more excited than Sam when going to middle school meant he could ride his bike to school.

Sam lost control of his bike for a minute. His balance was off, and for a second he couldn't tell which way was up. He heard the car's horn blast and closed his eyes as he squeezed his breaks and felt himself go sideways. Hot wind from the engine of the car pushed by him. When he opened his eyes, he was lying on his side, bike still between his legs, no car in view. He stayed there for a moment, feeling for injuries, decided he felt fine, and carefully picked himself and his bike up. He brushed off, remounted, and continued his ride home. *I've gotta tell Ben to tell his mom to slow down—she could've hit me!* He thought to himself.

He pulled his bike up to the side door and propped it against the wall, letting himself inside. No one was home, but Frodo was there, waiting as always, tail wagging so hard his whole body was vibrating.

"Hi boy!" Sam hugged his old friend around the neck, breathing in the smell of dog fur, which always reminded him of sunshine. "Let me get a snack and then I've got a game to show you!"

They were outside in the back yard, Sam throwing a tennis ball he'd found under his bed, when he heard voices from inside the house. He couldn't wait to show his parents what he'd taught Frodo.

"Why is the back door open?" His father's voice called. It sounded different, like something was wrong.

Both Mr. and Mrs. Hardin appeared at the back door. They were huddled together, looking pale, fragile. They saw Frodo. "How'd you get out, boy?" Mr. Hardin called, his voice slightly hoarse. "Come back inside, now."

But Sam wanted to show his parents the game. "Look at this!" he shouted, whistling loudly to get Frodo's attention. "See the ball? Get it!" and he threw it, a little harder than he'd meant to. It went bouncing out of the yard and into the woods at the edge of their property. Frodo barked once and went to fetch.

"Frodo, come here!" Mr. Hardin yelled, but the dog ignored him. He turned to his wife, who'd covered her face with both hands and was crying, her shoulders shaking. "Go on and sit down," he said, rubbing her back. "I'll get him."

He took slow steps across the yard, calling out, "Frodo! Here boy! Frodo!" moving in the direction he'd seen the dog go. Suddenly he heard a high whistle, and what sounded like an echo of his son's voice shouting, "Over here! Frodo, over here!" Catching his breath raggedly, he stumbled forward through the underbrush and into the dense foli age of the woods. He could hear the sounds of movement ahead and followed them all the way to the stream. At one point he thought he heard Sam laughing, answered by a happy yip from Frodo.

"Frodo?" Coming at last within sight of the small stream that defined the back edge of their property, he saw Frodo lying down, tail wagging, a yellow tennis ball in his mouth. He knelt beside the dog. "I figured you'd be waiting by the door when we got home," he murmured, stroking the dog's head. "You always wait by the door.... you always wait..." his voice died away, and silent tears began to fall from his eyes onto the dog's shoulder and paws. "He's not coming home today, boy," he stuttered. "He's not coming home." Mr. Hardin bowed his head and wept.

Frodo smelled his boy's smell on the ball in his mouth. He felt his presence in the air around him, and he knew that that was the last game they would play for a while.

Now it was Sam's turn to wait for Frodo to come home.

13

THE WESTERN WOODS

It was all Caden's fault.

If he hadn't dared me in front of the other guys, I wouldn't be here right now, wasting my time, taking the long way home through the woods.

Luke shook his head and kicked at a dead leaf. Caden had been his best friend since first grade, but lately he'd been a real jerk. It seemed like he would do anything to make the guys laugh, including throwing Luke under the bus.

"You shoulda heard her," they were sitting at their usual lunch table together. "'Don't walk through the western woods after the Equinox—the demons that haunt there will steal your soul!'" He'd hunched his shoulders up and used a wicked-witch voice that didn't really sound anything like Luke's grandmother.

"We were just kids," Luke had tried to lighten things. "She was trying to keep us out of trouble, that's all."

But the other guys hadn't bought it, and Caden ended up daring him to prove that he didn't believe in his grandmother's crazy stories.

Luke was still fuming, though at the time he'd tried not to let the guys see how angry he was.

How could he do that? How could he make fun of Gran when he knew the family situation? And tonight of all nights!

When they were little kids, Caden had adored Gran. He always wanted to play at Luke's house. He'd ask her to tell stories, abandoning whatever they were doing to sit and listen, asking his stupid questions, like he really believed it all.

Even just last year he'd said, "It's so cool that she's different. I wish my parents were Wiccans."

"She's not a Wiccan, she's just...Gran."

"Whatever, just so I wouldn't have to go to church."

I guess it's not 'so cool' any more, jerk.

Gran would be furious if she found out what he was doing. She took her stories seriously, and expected him to, as well.

He intended to make sure she would never know about this whole stupid thing.

He also intended to start avoiding Caden. He was sick of the way he'd been acting since they started high school. No friendship was worth putting up with this garbage.

The sound of scuffling in the leaves caught his attention, and he turned around. He expected to see a squirrel or deer. Instead, he caught Caden trying to duck behind a tree, a yard or so behind him.

"What are you doing?"

"Awww, I was going to sneak up on you," Caden came out from behind the tree grinning. "To video your reaction—thought the guys would get a kick out of it."

"Nice." Luke turned his back on him and began walking.

"Come on, Luke!" he could hear Caden running to catch up. "Why are you such a grouch these days? It's just a little joke—"

"Because it's not funny!" He gave Caden a shove. "I don't know you think it is, but it's not, and I've had it." He turned away, but Caden grabbed his arm.

"Hey!" The laughter was gone from his voice. "I'm sorry, okay? It's just..."

Luke yanked away from him and folded his arms, balling his fists. "Just what?"

Caden bent over to pick up a long stick and started poking at the ground. "I don't know. I mean, they all like you—you don't have to work at it, they just think you're cool automatically." He broke the stick in half. "I don't have your…way of acting like you don't care, you know?" he threw the stick pieces away. "I gotta do something to make them like me, too. So…"

"Are you telling me that you're being a total jerk because you think it will make you more popular?" Luke let his words drip with disgust. "Way to be a little girl about it, Caden. Very manly." He started walking again. At first he thought Caden would let him go on alone, but eventually he heard footsteps behind him.

They walked for a while, nothing but the sound of their feet scuffling through the underbrush. Finally, feeling calmer, Luke spoke.

"Why'd you have to make fun of Gran, though? I could take it if you want to tease me, but why Gran? What'd she ever do to you?"

Caden didn't answer at first. Then he jogged to catch up and walked beside Luke.

"I don't know." He sounded actually sad about it, and Luke cut him a side glance. "I'm sorry, okay?"

Luke just grunted, but it did make him feel better.

It was an hour's walk to get through the woods, and twilight was falling fast around them. Most of the leaves were gone from the trees, but it was still darker than it would've been out in the open. An owl made its lonely call from a distant tree.

"I think we're about halfway through," Caden said quietly. "Your gran will kill you if she finds out where you are."

"I know."

"Do you think…" Caden began, paused, then tried again. "I wonder why she tells those stories about these woods? Do you think it was really just to scare us when we were little, so we wouldn't wander in and get lost?"

Luke shook his head. "That was part of it, but Gran doesn't say things she doesn't believe. She told me that a couple of kids went missing from here when she was growing up, and they never found them."

"But it was probably like a kidnapping or serial killer or something," Caden sounded hopeful. "Or maybe they fell in a well."

"Gran believes it was evil spirits. Demons."

There was a sound off to their right that made them stop and listen.

"What was that?" Caden whispered.

"Not sure," Luke answered. "Let's keep going."

They walked faster, but it felt to Luke like they were walking through mud, their steps getting them nowhere.

"Did you hear that?" Caden grabbed his arm.

"What?"

"That sound---it was like someone moaning or something."

"Mmm-hmm. Probably just another owl." It hadn't sounded like any owl he'd ever heard, but he didn't want to admit it.

Something dropped out of the trees ahead of them, slightly to the left. They heard it breaking branches, felt the muffled thud when it hit the ground. They froze, and for a moment there was nothing, no movement, no sounds.

Then it screamed.

"Run!" Luke grabbed Caden's shirt collar and pulled him away.

Caden didn't waste his breath answering.

They ran furiously, jumping over logs and scrubby bushes, dodging trees and low branches. Behind them they could hear it in pursuit, a loping, galloping sound punctuated by wet snuffles and weird chuckling gurgles, as if it was amused with the chase.

THUD.

Another scream, this one higher, angrier, impatient. Now there were two shuffling somethings behind them. Caden and Luke could hear them chortling back and forth, like a weird conversation.

"I can't—keep---running—" Caden was gasping for breath.

"C'mon," Luke panted, "we've got to be close to the edge of the woods—we're almost out!"

"No—Luke—" Caden stumbled and fell to one knee. Luke stopped and grabbed his wrist, pulled him up, looked into the shadows behind them.

"Caden not now! I can hear them—they're getting closer—we've got to keep going!"

"What are they?" Caden's voice sounded like a small, frightened child's. He pushed himself up and started running again. "Is it bears?"

Luke didn't want to waste breath talking, but he needed Caden to be calm.

"Probably a couple of pit bulls escaped from someone's yard—they'll lose interest soon if we just keep going."

But he knew they weren't anyone's dogs.

Gran had told him more than she'd told Caden. She'd explained about the Ekimmu demons, who came before the Pilgrims, before the Dutch settlers, with the first tribes of men from far away continents who walked the land eons ago. Ancient, evil spirits, they fed on the misery and fear of humans, toyed with them like cats with mice, before sucking their life force away and turning them to dust. There were few places for them to hide in the modern world, she said, but forgotten tracts of dark forest like this one drew them.

That's what happened to those children who went missing. The police wouldn't listen, but I went to the woods in the spring and found all that was left of them, their sacred dust.

She'd told him about sprinkling their ashes into the brook that ran through the woods near the northern border.

No evil spirit can cross moving water, so their remains were safe and taken back into the world of sunlight and peace.

She'd told him what to look out for, too.

They are not designed for this world, so they are clumsy, she'd said, *and stupid though cunning. Do not underestimate them, do not listen to their foul language. You will feel a hot wind if they get too close, and you will smell brimstone.*

The only thing to do, she had told him again and again, is to run. *There is no fighting the Ekimmu, only escaping.*

Luke could hear Caden's breathing growing more ragged, and the bestial sounds behind them growing louder. Another crash, another otherworldly scream tore through the darkening woods, and a third joined the hunt.

"Is that another one?!" Caden sounded like he was on the edge of panic.

"It's all right," Luke panted, trying to smile sideways at him. "Probably just echoes."

Caden just whimpered. Behind them the creatures cackled and jeered.

Luke was thinking about the two kids who'd disappeared. He'd never really believed Gran's story about finding their dust. She could be pretty spooky about things sometimes, and he knew better than to ignore her, but he always thought she was just trying to scare him away from the woods the way other grown-ups scare their kids about crossing the street against the light.

Now he wasn't so sure.

Suddenly he remembered what she'd said about scattering their dust. *No evil spirit can cross moving water.*

He looked wildly around, trying to figure out where in the woods they were, and which way was north. He knew moss grew on the north side of trees and tried to figure out which way they were heading.

"Caden," he gasped, hope surging in him. "We need to get to the creek. We need to start heading north—that's to the left a little. Stay with me, okay?"

Caden just sucked air in raggedly for a minute. "But that's longer—let's go straight and get out of here!"

Luke heard a smattering of laughter behind them and thought he could smell something foul. *If I can smell them, they're too close.*

"No, Caden, you have to trust me. Dogs hate water," he hoped Caden was too frightened to think clearly about what he was saying. "If we cross the creek they'll stop—just stay with me!"

He turned his feet northward, keeping an eye on Caden, and an ear on the trio of demons.

For a few minutes it seemed like they were going deeper into the woods, and Caden whimpered again, "Luuuke!"

Then he saw something ahead—a flash, a glimmer of light. He waited until he was sure, then yelled to Caden, "I see it! Look up there

—you can see light reflecting on the water! Come on, Caden, we're almost there!"

The ghoulish melee behind them must've seen it too, because their weird chuckles became yelps, and he could hear their footfalls coming quicker. The stench of rotten eggs made him want to gag.

"God, what is that?" Caden was slowing down. "I can't breathe!"

"Forget about it!" Luke grabbed his shoulder and pushed him forward. "Just run—you can breathe on the other side of the water—now GO!"

He could hear the soft sound of water bubbling over stones, see it clearly just a few yards ahead. The Ekimmu were really running now, and a couple of times Luke felt something hot brush against the back of his neck, more than air but less than physical touch.

He shuddered, glancing at Caden. He saw him begin to smile as they sprinted the last few feet, then slip and fall.

"Luke!" He shrieked, sliding backward, his hands scrabbling in the dirt, looking for something to hold onto. "Help!"

Pivoting midstride, he dove for Caden's outstretched arm, grabbing his wrist with both hands. His heels dug into the soft undergrowth as he leaned backward, pulling with everything he had left. For a moment he thought he was losing hold, felt Caden's skin slipping beneath his fingers, heard him groaning—and then they let go.

"Come on!" He knew there was no time to waste. Luke jumped to his feet, grabbing Caden around the waist. Hooking his right arm over his shoulders he pulled him to the edge of the creek.

"Jump!"

It was wide here, and they landed knee-deep in water about three feet short of the far bank. Still hanging on, Luke dragged them both the last few feet and up onto the muddy flats on the other side.

Caden shoved him away and flopped backward, panting, holding his side and whimpering. "I can't run, it hurts too much, I can't run any more, Luke, I can't..."

Luke was staring into the darkness on the opposite side of the water. It was like seeing a black fog, with shapes and hints of figures poking through here and there. The feral cries of anger and defeat gradually began to sound more like angry birds, the hissing of a 'possum, the screech of an owl, fading into the night.

"That was the worst thing I've ever smelled," Caden said a few minutes later, sitting up, still holding his side. "What the hell was that? Do you really think it was some dogs?"

Luke dropped his head and rubbed his eyes, drawing a deep breath, relief washing over him. He stood up and offered his hand.

"I don't know." He heard his own voice shake slightly. "Maybe you were right, and it was bears."

Caden got up, wincing in pain, limping slightly as they began to walk. They turned their backs on the creek and continued going north. Now they could see stars peeking through the branches overhead and hear the sounds of traffic on nearby roads.

"Do you think we should report it to someone?"

Luke shrugged. "I don't know." He sure wasn't going to tell Gan about it.

Caden chuckled dryly. "Well, if I ever needed any proof that cross country wasn't for me, I think I got it tonight! I've never run so much in my life—this stitch in my side is killing me."

They walked quietly for a while.

"Listen," Caden said when they stood at the edge of the woods, looking at Broadview Road. "I'm sorry. I mean it. I shouldn't have said all that stuff to the guys. I'll tell them—"

"Forget about it," Luke said. He looked at his phone. "It's 5:30. I've got to get home to help Gran with the trick-or-treaters. You know how we always get a lot."

"She puts out all those carved pumpkins and stuff—the kids love that. Hey," Caden looked down, shoving his hands in his pockets, "want some company? My neighborhood's usually pretty dead. I could, you know, help out…"

"Weren't you and the guys going to get together? Tom said something about TP-ing the trees in the school parking lot."

"Nah," Caden looked away, then back at Luke, making eye contact. "I'd rather hang with you and your gran tonight. If that's okay, I mean."

Luke shrugged. "Sure. We'd better get moving, though. Trick-or-treating starts at 6:00."

"Hey Luke?"

"Yeah?"

Caden ran his hand through his hair and shook his head. "Seriously, what was that? You got me away, but it didn't feel like dogs or bears when it was pulling on me. It was…hot. And—*whew*!" he waved his hand in front of his face and wrinkled his nose. "I've never smelled anything like that!"

"Brimstone," Luke said. "I think that was brimstone."

A block away from Gran's house, a few early trick-or-treaters were marching up and down the street, ringing doorbells and holding out empty bags. Under a street light Caden stopped walking suddenly.

"Um, does brimstone do this?" he pointed to his right ankle. The bottom of his pant leg was wrinkled and browned, ragged at the edge, seared. They both stared, silent.

Luke cleared his throat. "Let's not mention this, okay? I wouldn't want Gran to…worry."

Caden frowned. "But maybe she might, you know, know something about it? She always told us to stay away from those woods…"

Luke shook his head. "Just…don't tell her. At least not tonight, okay?"

Caden looked at him for a long minute, then shrugged. "Whatever you say. She's your grandmother." They started walking again, closing in on the house. "But sometime I think we should ask some questions, find out more. Don't you?"

Luke didn't answer. He knew all he wanted to know about the Ekimmu and their dark world, and he knew he would never again walk through those woods during the dark months between equinoxes.

Acknowledgements

I am grateful to my many readers, who helped me create and compile this collection of stories: to Beren and Amelia my children, Judy and Paul my parents, and Ron my husband. Their feedback, questions, suggestions and cheerleading are the bread and butter of my work. I must also thank the many people whose ghost stories I have read since childhood, though I don't remember them all and can't name them. Their influence has guided and informed me here. In particular I am thankful for a small volume of "true" ghost stories I picked up while waiting for a ferry in Scotland, in 1993. "Scottish Ghost Stories" by Elliott O'Donnell kindled and defined my love for true ghost stories, ghost hunting, ghost books, and tales of the supernatural, and is the original inspiration for this volume.

About the Author

Elisabeth Wathen is a teacher, writer, poet, and musician. She lives with her husband and a loving orange tabby cat in their historic (and probably haunted) farmhouse, teaching and writing in the peace and beauty of the Catskills in Upstate New York.

www.ingramcontent.com/pod-product-compliance
Lightning Source LLC
Chambersburg PA
CBHW071616150726
48000CB00004B/1754